The Kenz Collection

M.A. Hagan

Jug Run Press

Contents

Chapter 1

Raisa pulled into the Millers' farm driveway at exactly seven forty-five, as she had every third Tuesday for the past fifteen years. Punctuality was a small thing, perhaps, but it was hers. In a world that seemed increasingly determined to spin beyond anyone's control, arriving when she said she would arrive felt like a form of dignity.

Elizabeth was waiting on the porch, her dark blue dress and black apron as crisp as the October air, her hands busy with some small task even in these borrowed moments. Raisa recognized the motion; shelling late beans, probably, into the ceramic bowl balanced on her lap. Elizabeth's hands were never truly idle, always finding productive work in the spaces between other work. It was one thing Raisa appreciated about her, this understanding that stillness and industry weren't opposites.

Raisa turned off the engine and stepped out, feeling the familiar pull in her right knee that the coming winter would make worse. Sixty-seven wasn't old, she reminded herself, just experienced. Settled. Her body knew its rhythms now, knew to move carefully in the morning cold before everything loosened and warmed.

"Good morning," Elizabeth called, her voice carrying the slight lilt that marked her Amish background, vowels rounded in ways that still charmed Raisa's ear after all these years. "Right on time, as always."

"Morning," Raisa replied, climbing the porch steps to help with the bowl. "We've got good weather for the drive. Dr. Patterson's office by nine-fifteen, you'll be done by ten-thirty if he stays on schedule, and we can stop at that fabric store you mentioned on the way back if you'd like."

Elizabeth's smile deepened, lines creasing around her eyes in patterns Raisa had memorized without meaning to. "You have it all planned."

"That's what you pay me for." But Raisa's tone was warm, the gentle mockery of long friendship. They both knew the fee Elizabeth paid barely covered gas money. These drives were something else, something that had grown beyond transaction into the comfortable territory of a chosen routine.

They settled into the van, Elizabeth placing her bowl of shelled beans carefully on the floor between her feet, handling the seatbelt with the slight hesitation of someone who still found motorized transportation faintly unnatural even after decades of necessary use. Raisa waited for the click before starting the engine, a small patience that cost her nothing.

The farm receded in the rearview mirror: the white farmhouse, white barn, and the garden plots lying fallow now that frost had come and gone. Samuel would be at morning chores, their five children dispersed to their various tasks and schooling. The thought of that household's organized chaos made Raisa smile before she redirected her attention to the road.

Route 19 stretched ahead. She'd driven it so many times she could navigate it by feel: the slight dip a quarter mile past the Yoder farm, the curve that tightened more than it appeared, the spot where the morning sun would glare directly into her eyes come summer but now, in October, it slanted harmlessly to the south. Knowledge like this accumulated slowly, deposited in careful layers. You couldn't rush toward it; you could only show up, again and again, until the knowing became part of you.

They drove in comfortable silence for the first few miles. Elizabeth watched the fields pass, her attention on seasonal changes Raisa had learned to notice through her. There was the way the remaining corn stubble caught light differently than summer's green had, how the tree line showed its bones now. Elizabeth noticed things, observing them with the same attention she brought to her herbs, to her journals full of careful notes about what grew when, what combinations worked, what the old knowledge said, and what her own experimentation had proven or disproven.

"How has your week been?" Elizabeth asked finally, her tone genuinely inquiring rather than merely polite.

Raisa considered the question while navigating the turn onto Baker Road. How had her week been? Busy. Productive. She'd driven Mrs. Peachy to her sister's funeral on Monday, the Stoltzfus family to a wedding in Lancaster on Thursday, and young Jacob Lapp to his first day at the furniture workshop on Friday. She'd maintained her schedule, arrived promptly, charged fairly, caused no problems and solved several.

"Steady," she said. "Enough work to keep me occupied, but not so much that I couldn't manage it." The truth, but not the whole truth.

"That's good," Elizabeth said, and let the silence return without pushing. This was another thing Raisa valued; her comfort with quiet, her willingness to let conversations breathe instead of forcing them into awkward fullness.

They passed the Beiler farm, where laundry already snapped on the lines despite the early hour. The Fisher place, where the youngest boy waved from his perch on the fence. The miles accumulated steadily, marked by familiar landmarks that required no comment.

"And Mackenzie?" Elizabeth asked. "How is your granddaughter?"

The question landed with more weight than Elizabeth could have intended. Raisa felt her hands tighten on the steering wheel, watched her knuckles pale slightly before she consciously relaxed her grip. How was Kenz? Eleven years old. Smart. Creative. Loving. Utterly exhausting.

"She's fine," Raisa said. "Growing like a weed."

"It's good that you spend time with her." Elizabeth's tone was carefully neutral, but Raisa heard the question underneath. They hadn't talked about this directly, but Elizabeth knew, the way friends who paid attention always knew, that Raisa's relationship with her granddaughter had become complicated in ways that caused Raisa quiet pain.

The silence stretched. Raisa could leave it there, could redirect the conversation to something easier, could maintain the pleasant surface of their morning drive. But something in her was tired. Tired of holding things carefully in place, tired of presenting only her most competent self, tired of the loneliness that came from never admitting struggle.

"She was over last week," Raisa heard herself say. "She wanted to help me with the laundry."

Elizabeth made a small, encouraging sound, the kind that invited continuation without demanding it.

"I had whites soaking in the utility sink," Raisa continued, watching the road but seeing her bathroom instead with the pink-tinged water, and Kenz's stricken face, the new red shirt she'd thrown in with everything pale. "She thought she'd be helpful and start a load in the washer. Didn't check what she was adding."

"Ah," Elizabeth said.

"Everything came out pink. My good blouses, the tablecloth my mother gave me, the pillowcases I've had for twenty years." She tried to keep her voice level, factual, but she heard the edge creeping in anyway. "She felt terrible, of course. Nearly cried. But the damage was done."

"These things happen with children," Elizabeth offered.

"She's eleven, not six." The words came sharper than Raisa intended. She took a breath and tried again. "I know she didn't mean to. I know she was trying to help. But she never slows down enough to think first. She just acts, immediately, with all that energy in whatever direction catches her attention. And I—"

Raisa stopped herself, but Elizabeth waited, patient as stone.

"I love her," Raisa finished quietly. "Of course I love her. She's my granddaughter. But lately, every time she visits, I spend the next three days recovering from the damage."

There. She'd said it. The thing that made her feel small and mean and ungenerous. The truth she couldn't quite admit even to herself in the dark hours of early morning.

"It's not just the laundry," she continued, the confession gaining momentum now that it had started. "Two weeks ago, she knocked over my tea set. The antique one, the only thing I have from my grandmother. She was gesturing while talking. Her whole body is always involved in every sentence, and her elbow caught the shelf. Three cups and the teapot, shattered."

Elizabeth made a sympathetic sound.

"Early last month she was helping me in the garden and pulled up every single dahlia shoot, thinking they were grass." Raisa's voice had gone flat now, reciting damages like an insurance claim. "Years of dividing and nurturing, specific varieties I'd collected. Gone in twenty minutes because she wasn't paying attention to what I'd shown her, what I'd explained carefully before we even went outside."

"The ADHD makes focusing difficult for her," Elizabeth said gently.

"I know." She did know. Intellectually, she understood that Kenz's brain worked differently, that the medications helped but didn't eliminate the challenges, that her granddaughter's chaos wasn't willful misbehavior. "I know it's not her fault. That's what makes it harder, somehow. I can't even be properly angry because she's trying so hard, and she feels terrible when things go wrong, and she loves me and wants my approval so desperately it breaks my heart."

The words kept coming. "Her mother called me yesterday and asked if Kenz could come over tomorrow to help with some yard work. She said it so hopefully: Kenz had been talking about wanting to help Grandma with the garden, wanting to make up for the dahlias. And I said yes, because what else could I say? But I've been dreading it. Actually dreading time with my own granddaughter. What kind of person does that make me?"

"It makes you human," Elizabeth said.

Raisa shook her head, though whether in denial or acknowledgment even she wasn't sure. They'd reached the highway now, and she merged into light traffic with practiced ease, grateful for the task that gave her hands and eyes something to do.

"My mother drank," Raisa said after a long pause, the words emerging from somewhere deep and usually locked. "Not socially. Not a glass of wine with dinner. She drank the way some people breathe. By the time I was Kenz's age, I'd learned to read the signs. How her movements changed as the evening progressed, how her voice transformed, how the entire atmosphere of our house shifted depending on whether she'd had two drinks or five."

Elizabeth listened, her attention absolute but undemanding.

"I learned to control what I could control," she continued. "Keep things quiet. Keep things orderly. Don't provoke chaos, because chaos meant danger, meant things breaking, meant uncertainty and fear and having to manage situations no child should have to manage."

She'd never said this out loud before, not in so many words. Not to her daughter, Claire, not to her late husband, certainly not to herself.

"I thought I'd dealt with all that," she said. "Decades of being a functional adult, of building a life that worked, of being the reliable person other people count on. I thought I'd moved past letting childhood fears dictate adult reactions. But when Kenz comes over with all that energy, all that beautiful, exhausting, relentless chaos, I feel something in me clench up tight. It's like I'm eleven again, trying to keep the world from spinning out of control."

"Our early patterns run deep," Elizabeth said. "Deeper than we usually want to admit."

They drove in silence for a while. Raisa felt simultaneously lighter and more exposed, as if confession had removed protective weight but left her vulnerable to elements she'd forgotten how to weather.

"I don't want to be the grandmother who can't enjoy her granddaughter," she said finally. "I don't want to count down the hours until she leaves, or feel relief when her mother picks her up, or brace myself before visits like I'm preparing for something to endure rather than enjoy. But that's what's happening, and I don't know how to stop it."

"Have you talked to her mother about it?"

Raisa's laugh came out bitter. "And say what? That her daughter is too much for me to handle? That I'm not capable of managing a few hours with an eleven-year-old? Claire is already overwhelmed trying to balance work and Kenz's needs. The last thing she needs is me admitting I can't cope either."

Elizabeth was quiet for a moment, her attention seemingly on the landscape passing outside her window; the strip malls giving way to more developed areas, the signs indicating they were approaching the medical complex.

"You know I work with herbs," Elizabeth said finally.

She glanced over, surprised by the apparent non sequitur. "Of course."

"My grandmother taught me, and her grandmother taught her. Knowledge passed down through generations, combined with what I've learned from books, from experimentation, from paying attention to what works."

Elizabeth's voice had taken on a different quality. It was still gentle, but with an undercurrent of something more intentional. "People come to me with various struggles. Anxiety. Sleeplessness. Nervous energy that needs calming."

Raisa felt something shift within her, though she couldn't name it yet.

"I have a compound," she continued carefully. "Something I've made variations of for people who struggle with racing thoughts, and with an energy that outpaces their ability to direct it productively. It supports the body's own rhythms, helping create a sense of calm focus."

"For children?" Raisa heard herself ask.

"I've used similar formulations for adults dealing with various forms of restlessness." Elizabeth's tone was precise now, the way it got when she discussed her herbalism: part scientist, part practitioner of old knowledge. "The principle is the same. It's working with the body's natural tendencies rather than against them."

They'd reached the medical complex. Raisa pulled into the parking lot, found a space near the entrance Dr. Patterson's office occupied, and turned off the engine.

"I'm not suggesting more medication," Elizabeth said. "And I would never presume to interfere with what Kenz's doctors have already prescribed. But if you felt it might help during her more challenging moments, I could prepare something. Something gentle that might take the edge off the most intense energy."

Raisa sat still, her hands resting on the steering wheel though the van was no longer moving. Part of her recognized this as the moment she should ask questions, should carefully consider, should apply the same caution she brought to all decisions. But another part, the exhausted part that had been dreading tomorrow's visit, the part that remembered pink pillowcases and shattered teacups and destroyed gardens, felt something dangerous crystallizing into hope.

"Would it..." she started, then paused, trying to frame the question properly. "Would it hurt her?"

"No," Elizabeth said firmly. "I would never offer something that could cause harm. It's made from plants, carefully measured and prepared. At worst, it would do nothing at all. At best, it might provide a few hours of calmer focus."

"And you've used this successfully before?"

"Variations of it, yes. For people dealing with anxiety, with racing thoughts, with a nervous energy that needed gentling."

Raisa turned to look directly at her friend . Elizabeth's face was open, concerned, clearly sincere in her offer to help. There was no judgment there, no condemnation for Raisa's struggles. Just the same practical kindness Elizabeth brought to all her interactions.

"If you're interested," Elizabeth said, "I could prepare a small amount. You'd need to be careful with the dosage: one drop, no more, mixed into food or drink. And it's important that you tell her what you're giving her, that she knows and consents. The body responds better to things when the mind understands and accepts them."

Raisa nodded, filing away the instructions even as part of her brain noted them with something like warning bells she wasn't quite ready to hear.

"I'll have my appointment now," Elizabeth said, gathering her purse and opening her door. "Think about it while I'm inside. No pressure either way. But the offer stands if you'd like help."

She disappeared into the medical building, moving with the slightly stiff gait of someone whose joints protested chilly mornings. Raisa watched her go, then sat alone in the van with the engine ticking as it cooled and her thoughts spinning in directions she recognized as potentially dangerous but couldn't quite bring herself to redirect.

The problem was that Elizabeth's offer made sense. It wasn't like drugging someone. Not really. It was herbs, natural compounds, things people had used for centuries to support health and well-being. Elizabeth was knowledgeable, careful, and had used similar preparations successfully before. And it would just be for tomorrow, just to help make the visit manageable, just to give both Raisa and Kenz a chance to enjoy each other's company without the constant undercurrent of chaos and damage control.

Raisa pulled out her phone and scrolled absently through messages she'd already read, anything to occupy her hands while her mind circled. She thought about tomorrow, about Kenz arriving with her characteristic explosive enthusiasm, and about her garden beds with perennials that needed careful dividing and mulching before winter came. She imagined trying to explain which plants to keep and which to remove, watching Kenz's attention scatter to an interesting beetle or rock and come back to find more destruction despite the best intentions.

Or, she imagined the same scenario with Kenz just slightly calmer, slightly more focused, able to listen and retain, and work carefully. Able to enjoy the time together without the exhaustion that always followed.

When Elizabeth emerged forty-five minutes later, Raisa already knew her answer. She waited until they were back on the highway, heading toward the fabric store Elizabeth had mentioned, before speaking.

"That compound you mentioned," she said, keeping her voice carefully neutral. "If it's not too much trouble, I think I'd like to try it."

Elizabeth nodded. "I can prepare something this evening, have it ready for you before you leave." She paused, then added with careful emphasis, "Remember: only one drop, and make sure Kenz knows what you're giving her. Consent matters, even when we're trying to help. Especially then."

"Of course," Raisa said, though even as she spoke, she felt uneasy. "I understand."

They finished the drive in companionable silence, stopping at the fabric store where Elizabeth selected materials for a quilt one of her daughters was making, then heading back toward the farm. The fall landscape rolled past, beautiful in its decline, everything preparing for dormancy, for the season of rest that preceded renewal.

When they pulled into the farm drive, Elizabeth asked Raisa to wait a moment while she went inside. She returned carrying a small glass vial, no bigger than Raisa's thumb, filled with liquid the color of spring leaves. She placed it carefully in Raisa's palm, and it was surprisingly cool to the touch.

"One drop," Elizabeth repeated. "Mixed into food or drink. And tell her what you're giving—"

"I will," Raisa interrupted, not wanting to hear the warning again because hearing it meant acknowledging the part of her that was already planning to skip that instruction. "Thank you, Elizabeth. I really appreciate this."

Elizabeth looked at her for a long moment, and Raisa had the uncomfortable feeling of being seen more clearly than she wanted, but then her friend simply nodded and stepped back from the van.

"I hope it helps," she said. "And Raisa? Be careful. Sometimes the help we think we need isn't the help that actually serves us."

Raisa thanked her again and drove away, watching the farm recede in her rearview mirror until the road curved and trees blocked the view. The vial sat in her cardigan pocket, a small weight she touched every few minutes, just to confirm its presence.

It was just herbs; she told herself. Just a little help to make tomorrow manageable. Elizabeth had said it was safe, saying she'd used similar preparations before. One drop, carefully measured, would do no harm and might do considerable good. It might give her and Kenz the peaceful afternoon together they both deserved, and it might prove that Raisa could be the grandmother she wanted to be, patient, present, and enjoying rather than enduring.

By the time she pulled into her own driveway, the unease had mostly subsided, replaced by something that felt almost like relief. She had a solution now, a way to manage what had felt unmanageable. Tomorrow would be different. Tomorrow would be better.

She took the vial inside and placed it carefully in her bathroom cabinet, behind the vitamin bottles, where it would be safe but accessible. Then she called her daughter, Claire, to confirm that yes, Kenz should come over tomorrow morning, and yes, they'd do some garden work together, and no, it was no imposition at all. She was looking forward to it.

And the strange thing was, she realized as she ended the call, it was true. For the first time in months, she was actually looking forward to time with her granddaughter. The anticipation felt clean, uncomplicated by dread or anxiety, or the bracing sensation of preparing for something to endure.

She had Elizabeth's compound. She had a plan. Everything would be fine.

The vial sat in the cabinet, small and green, and full of promise. Raisa closed the cabinet door and went to make herself dinner, humming slightly, already thinking through tomorrow's tasks. Which perennials needed dividing. How she'd explain the work to Kenz. How peaceful it would be when her granddaughter could actually focus and listen and work carefully for once.

She was helping her; she told herself. That's what grandmothers did. They helped. And if she had to bend Elizabeth's warnings just slightly to make that help effective, well, surely the end justified such small adjustments to the means. Kenz didn't need to know about one tiny drop in her afternoon cookie. What mattered was the result: a good day together, positive memories instead of disasters, the relationship Raisa wanted rather than the exhausting reality it had become.

Outside her kitchen window, the October afternoon faded toward evening. The garden beds waited, full of perennials that needed tending before winter arrived. Tomorrow she and Kenz would work on them together, and it would be good. She was certain of it.

The vial sat in the bathroom cabinet like a promise.

Or a warning.

She interpreted it as the former.

Chapter 2

Raisa went to bed that night and slept better than she had in weeks. She had been up since six, organizing her garden tools, reviewing which perennials needed division, and planning the workflow. The beds had been carefully designed over the years. Daylilies were in the back border, hostas in the shaded section near the fence, coneflowers and black-eyed Susans in the sunny middle ground. Each plant placed with intention, creating combinations of color and texture and bloom time that had taken seasons to perfect.

The work ahead was delicate. Dividing perennials required knowing where to cut, how to separate root systems without destroying them, which divisions were viable, and which were too small to survive winter. It was a task that demanded attention and care, and work she usually reserved for herself alone. But she'd wanted to include Kenz, wanted to share this knowledge, wanted an afternoon where they could work together productively.

She checked her watch. Nine forty-five. Kenz would arrive in fifteen minutes, which meant actually twenty to thirty minutes given Claire's relationship with punctuality. She didn't judge. She knew single parenting was exhausting, that mornings with Kenz involved chasing her through transitions, reminding her five times to put on shoes, and finding the glasses she'd set down somewhere and immediately forgotten.

The vial sat on her bathroom counter where she'd placed it that morning, just in case. But looking at it now in the clear daylight, Raisa felt a whisper of something uncomfortable. Elizabeth's words echoed: *Make sure Kenz knows what you're giving her. Consent matters.*

She picked up the vial and turned it in her fingers. The liquid inside caught the light, showing the green of new spring growth. It was so small. Surely something this small couldn't cause actual harm. And if it helped Kenz focus, if it made the afternoon manageable for both of them, wasn't that a kindness?

She slipped the vial into her cardigan pocket and went downstairs to wait.

Claire's car pulled into the driveway at 10:07, which was actually early by recent standards. She watched from the kitchen window as Kenz exploded from the passenger seat. There was no other word for it. The door flew open and her granddaughter emerged in a flurry of motion, already talking before her feet hit the pavement, gesturing with both hands while her mother called something after her that Kenz clearly wasn't hearing.

Strawberry-blonde hair escaped from a ponytail that had probably been neat twenty minutes ago. Thick-framed glasses were smudged and slightly crooked. Grass-stained knees visible through ripped jeans that might have been fashionably distressed or just authentically worn. With Kenz it was impossible to tell. She wore a striped t-shirt, already untucked on one side.

And despite everything, despite the dread of recent months, despite the broken heirlooms and ruined laundry and destroyed plants, she felt her heart expand with pure love. This was her granddaughter. This enthusiastic, chaotic, frustrating, beautiful child who was already running toward the door, already calling "Grandma! Grandma, I'm here! I brought my good gloves, the ones with the rubber grips. I remembered this time!"

She opened the door and was immediately engulfed in a hug that smelled like strawberry shampoo and something indefinably kid-flavored, sweet and slightly grubby.

"I'm so excited," Kenz said into her shoulder. "I've been thinking about the garden all week, I even watched some videos about dividing perennials, well, I started watching them, there was this really interesting one about root systems and did you know that some plants are basically immortal if you keep dividing them? They just keep going forever, which is kind of amazing when you think about it, like that plant could be older than both of us combined."

"Breathe, sweetheart," Raisa said, pulling back to smile at her. "We have all afternoon."

Kenz's mother had made it to the door, looking perpetually harried in the way of parents managing more than they had the capacity for. "Call if you need anything," she said to her own mother, though they both knew she wouldn't. "I'll be back at three. Kenz, remember what we talked about. Listen to Grandma, slow down, think before you act."

"I will, I promise, I'm going to be so careful, you'll see, Grandma's going to be so proud of me." She was already pulling toward the garden, vibrating with eagerness.

Her mother left with a grateful wave, and she was alone with her granddaughter and the October morning with several hours of work ahead that required precisely the kind of careful attention Kenz had never successfully demonstrated.

The vial sat in Raisa's pocket, a small weight she was acutely aware of. But not yet. Give it a chance first. Maybe today would be different.

The garden beds looked beautiful in the morning light, Raisa thought as they walked the perimeter together. Years of work were visible in the deliberate arrangement with its careful balance of texture and color.

"Okay," she said, stopping at the first bed. "Let me show you what we're doing. See these daylilies? They've been here for three years now, and they're getting crowded. When perennials get too dense, they stop blooming as well. So we need to dig them up, divide the roots, and replant the healthiest sections."

Kenz nodded vigorously, her whole upper body involved in the gesture. "Right, right, I saw that in the video. You have to separate the fans, that's what they're called, the leaf parts are fans."

"But the important thing," Raisa continued, needing to be clear before they started, "is knowing what to keep and what to remove. Not everything green is a plant we want. See here?" She pointed to a cluster of dandelion leaves growing between the daylilies. "These are weeds. They need to come out. But these," she touched the daylily shoots gently, "these we're keeping. Can you see the difference?"

"Sure, sure, the daylilies are longer and they grow in those fan shapes and the dandelions are jaggedy." Kenz reached out as she spoke, her hand moving in illustration, and nearly knocked over the bucket of tools Raisa had carefully arranged.

"Careful," she said, steadying it. "Let's work slowly and deliberately today, okay? This is delicate work."

"I know, I will, I'm going to be so careful, you won't believe how careful I'm going to be"

Raisa handed her a small trowel and a pair of gloves. "Start here with the weeding, just this section. Pull only the obvious weeds: the dandelions, the crabgrass, and anything that looks different from the daylilies. If you're not sure, ask me first. Don't just pull."

"Don't just pull, ask first. Got it." Kenz pulled on the gloves, wiggling her fingers. "These are good gloves, see, they have the grippy parts, Mom got them for me after I kept dropping stuff... Oh, look at that beetle! Grandma, come look, it's got the most amazing metallic shell, it's like green and copper at the same time--"

"Kenz. The weeding."

"Right, right, sorry." Kenz dropped to her knees in the garden bed with the same explosive energy she brought to everything. Her hands immediately started moving, pulling at green things without apparent discrimination.

Raisa watched for a moment, saw a dandelion successfully removed, then a blade of crabgrass, and felt herself relax slightly. Maybe this would be okay. Maybe---

Kenz's hand closed around a hosta shoot; mot a daylily. She was in the wrong section already. It was another hosta Raisa had been carefully nurturing for two seasons. A specific variety with blue-green leaves that would spread into a beautiful mound by next summer. The girl yanked, and the entire plant came up, roots and all.

"Kenz, no!" Raisa moved forward, but it was already done. The hosta lay in Kenz's muddy glove, roots dangling.

"Oh." Kenz stared at it. "Oh no. This wasn't a weed, was it?"

Raisa took a breath, held it, released it slowly. "No, sweetheart. That was a hosta. See how different the leaves are from what I showed you?"

"I'm sorry, I'm so sorry, I wasn't looking carefully enough. I just grabbed the green thing and pulled. I didn't mean to... Can we put it back? Can we replant it?" Kenz's voice had gone high and anxious, and her knee was bouncing even though she was kneeling, some part of her always in motion.

"We can try," Raisa said, though she knew the success rate wasn't good. The roots had torn when Kenz pulled. But she took the plant gently, dug a proper hole, settled it back in place and firmed the soil around it. "It's okay.

Mistakes happen. But this is why I need you to slow down and look before you pull. Really look. Can you do that?"

"Yes, absolutely, I promise, I'm going to look so carefully." Kenz was already turning back to the bed, her hands reaching.

"Wait." Raisa caught her shoulder. "Before you touch anything else, show me what you're about to pull. Point to it first, tell me what you think it is. Then I'll tell you if it's right."

Kenz's face brightened. "Okay, that's good, that's a good system. So this one," she pointed to an actual dandelion, "this is definitely a weed, right? The jagged leaves?"

"Correct."

"And this one is..." Kenz's finger hovered over a daylily, and Raisa saw her really looking this time, comparing it to the plant beside it. "This is a keeper. A daylily."

"Right. Good."

For approximately four minutes, the system worked. Kenz pointed, Raisa confirmed or corrected, weeds were successfully removed. Raisa felt the tightness in her chest ease slightly. They could do this. With enough structure and supervision, they could--

"Oh my gosh, Grandma, did you know that daylilies are edible? I was reading about it, well, I was reading about something else and there was a link about edible flowers and apparently you can eat daylily buds and they taste kind of like asparagus, or maybe green beans, the article wasn't totally clear, and I was thinking we could try it sometime, like have a whole meal made from the garden, that would be so cool, we could--"

While talking, Kenz's hands had kept moving, operating independently from her consciousness. She'd pulled four plants in a row: two weeds, one daylily shoot that Raisa had been planning to keep, and some kind of grass that might or might not have been intentional. Her attention was on her words, on the fascinating idea of edible flowers, while her hands followed their own chaotic logic.

"Kenz." Raisa's voice came out sharper than she intended. "Your hands. You're not looking."

Kenz glanced down at the pile of vegetation she'd accumulated, and her face fell. "Oh. Oh no. I did it again, didn't I? I was thinking about the edible flowers and I just kept pulling and I wasn't-- I'm sorry, Grandma, I'm really trying."

"I know you are." She knelt beside her, and sorted through the pulled plants. The daylily shoot was probably salvageable. She replanted it carefully, aware of Kenz watching with stricken attention. "But trying isn't enough if you're not aware of what your hands are doing. Your brain and your body need to be coordinated."

"I know. You're right. I'll be more careful." Kenz's knee bounced faster. Her fingers pulled at a loose thread on her jeans. Even sitting still, she was in constant motion, her energy looking for an outlet.

Raisa felt the weight of the vial in her pocket. Just one drop. Just enough to help coordinate that beautiful, exhausting energy into something focused and productive.

But not yet. They'd barely started. Give her more time.

"Let's try a different approach," she said, standing and brushing dirt from her knees. "Why don't you work on this section here," she indicated a patch that was entirely weeds, with nothing valuable to accidentally destroy, "and I'll work on the dividing. Just focus on pulling everything green in this area. It all needs to come out."

Kenz's face lit up. "I can do that! Pull everything, got it, that's easy."

She attacked the weedy section with ferocious energy, and for a while it actually worked. Raisa managed to divide two clumps of daylilies, separating the roots carefully, selecting the healthiest fans for replanting. The work was meditative, the kind of task she could lose herself in; the smell of earth, the satisfaction of seeing the tangle of roots come apart into individual viable plants, the knowledge that next summer these divisions would bloom.

She'd gotten through the second clump when she heard Kenz say, "Okay, I finished that section, what's next?"

Raisa looked up. The weedy patch was indeed clear, and so was the carefully planned section of hostas beside it. Every single plant had been pulled, dumped in an enthusiastic pile, roots exposed to the air and already beginning to dry out.

For a moment, Raisa couldn't speak. Those hostas represented three years of work. She'd started with one expensive specimen, divided it the first year into three plants, divided those the second year into nine. This year she'd been planning to divide again, creating enough to finally fill the entire shaded border the way she'd envisioned. Years of patient planning, of careful timing, of protecting the tender shoots from early spring slugs.

Gone. Yanked like weeds and piled like trash.

"Kenz." Her voice came out flat, carefully controlled. "Those were hostas. Those were all hostas. I showed you earlier what hostas look like."

Kenz stared at the pile, then at the empty section of garden, then back at Raisa. "But... but you said pull everything green in that section, I thought... I was just doing what you said--"

"I said this section." Raisa pointed to the weedy patch. "This specific area. Not the entire bed. Not everything you could reach."

"Oh." Kenz's voice got very small. "Oh, Grandma, I'm sorry, I wasn't... I didn't mean to. Can we replant them? Like the other one?"

Raisa looked at the pile. Some might survive if she worked quickly, if she got them back in the ground before the roots dried completely. But the careful arrangement was destroyed. The three-year plan demolished. And even if she saved some of the plants, it would set her back years. Years of patient work undone in - she checked her watch - twenty minutes.

"We can try," she said, though something in her chest felt tight. "Let me show you how to replant them properly."

They worked together for the next thirty minutes, Raisa digging holes and settling the traumatized hostas back into place while Kenz handed her plants and apologized in a constant anxious stream and asked questions about whether they'd be okay and whether Grandma was mad and what she could do to help fix it and had Raisa seen that article about plant communication, how they apparently share information through root systems, which was fascinating when you thought about it...

Raisa's patience was eroding like soil in heavy rain, wearing away in channels that kept getting deeper. She could feel it happening and couldn't stop it. Each plant she replanted felt like another small failure, another piece of evidence that this afternoon was going to be exactly like all the other visits, full of chaos and damage and barely controlled disaster.

The vial seemed to pulse in her pocket, though she knew that was impossible. Just a small bottle of liquid, sitting still and inert. But she was aware of it constantly now, the way you're aware of a lifeboat when you're treading water, not drowning yet but getting tired, wondering how much longer you can keep going.

"Okay," she said when the last hosta was back in the ground, survival uncertain. "Let's try something simpler. I need you to spread mulch around these plants, the ones I've just divided and replanted. Just mulch. Not pulling, not digging, just spreading the mulch evenly to help protect the roots for winter."

"I can definitely do that," Kenz said eagerly. "That's easy, just spreading, I'm really good at spreading, one time in art class we had to spread paint with these big brushes and I covered the whole paper really fast."

Raisa showed her how much mulch to use, how to spread it around but not touching the crown of the plant, where to draw the materials from the pile she'd had delivered last week. "Just like this. Slow and even. Can you do that?"

"Absolutely." Kenz grabbed a handful of mulch. She grabbed it, rather than using the small shovel Raisa had provided, and flung it toward the nearest plant with such enthusiasm that half of it scattered across the lawn and the rest buried the poor daylily completely.

"Kenz—no—gently—"

"Oops, sorry, too much, I'll fix it." Kenz reached to brush the mulch off and grabbed the plant itself instead, yanking it sideways, partially uprooting what Raisa had just carefully replanted.

Something hot and sharp spiked through Raisa's chest. Not quite anger. Something closer to despair mixed with a desperate, clawing need for this to stop, for Kenz to just slow down for five seconds, for the careening chaos to pause long enough for Raisa to catch her breath.

"Stop," she said. "Just stop touching things for a minute. Stand up and step back."

Kenz scrambled to her feet, mulch falling from her gloves, her expression crumpling. "I'm sorry, I was trying to help."

"I know." Raisa pressed her fingers against her temples, where a headache was beginning to build. "I know you're trying. But your kind of help is making more work, not less."

She heard the words come out and immediately regretted them. She saw them land on Kenz like stones, saw her granddaughter's face go carefully blank in that way that meant she was internalizing something painful. But she was too exhausted to take it back, to soften it, to find the gentler version of the truth.

They were only an hour into the visit. Two more hours stretched ahead, and Raisa's garden was already a disaster zone, and Kenz was still vibrating with unfocused energy that seemed to find the most destructive possible outlet no matter how carefully Raisa tried to direct it.

Her hand found the vial in her pocket and closed around it. She felt its smooth coolness against her palm.

Just one drop. Elizabeth had said it was safe. Just enough to help Kenz focus, to calm that relentless energy into something manageable. Just for this afternoon, just to get through the important work without any more destruction.

"I think we need a break," Raisa heard herself say.

Kenz followed her toward the house, uncharacteristically quiet, and Raisa tried not to look back at the garden, at the displaced hostas and the scattered mulch and the carefully planned beds now looking like a tornado had touched down in selected locations.

In the kitchen, making sandwiches would give her something to do with her hands. And cookies would give her an opportunity to make a decision she was increasingly certain was the only reasonable option left.

Just one drop. Just to help. Just this once.

The vial sat in her pocket like a promise, and Raisa felt herself reaching toward it the way drowning people reach toward air.

Chapter 3

"I'll bring out some cookies and lemonade."

Her granddaughter's face lit up with such pure delight that Raisa felt something twist beneath her ribs. "That sounds amazing! I'm so hungry, I didn't realize how hungry I was until you said cookies, and now I'm thinking about those chocolate chip ones you make, the ones with the sea salt on top. Are those the ones? I hope those are the ones."

"Come sit at the patio table when you're ready," Raisa said, already turning toward the kitchen before she could see more of that eager, trusting face.

Inside, her hands moved with their usual efficiency, laying out a small plate, selecting three cookies from the tin she'd baked two days ago. Not the chocolate chip. Something simpler. Oatmeal raisin. The kind that would mask any subtle taste the drop might carry, though Elizabeth had said the potion was nearly flavorless. A glass of lemonade from the pitcher in the refrigerator. A napkin folded beside the plate.

The vial sat on the counter where she'd placed it, small and green and filled with liquid the color of new spring growth. Just one drop, Elizabeth had said. One drop mixed into food or drink.

Raisa unscrewed the cap with steady fingers. The motion felt both momentous and utterly ordinary, no different from opening any bottle in her kitchen. Inside, the liquid caught the afternoon light filtering through the window above the sink.

And tell her what you're giving her. Consent matters.

Elizabeth's voice in her memory was clear and firm, impossible to ignore. Raisa's hand paused, the vial tilted over the cookie she'd selected; the middle one, slightly larger than its companions.

She could still stop. Could put the cap back on, return the vial to its hiding place, serve Kenz plain cookies and muddle through the rest of the afternoon with gritted teeth and mounting anxiety. She could call Claire early, admit that the visit wasn't working out, and that she couldn't handle Kenz's energy level today.

She could accept that as a failure and live with it, or she could help. She could give Kenz the gentle support Elizabeth had described, the calming focus that would let them actually enjoy the afternoon together. Just one drop of a harmless plant compound that Elizabeth used successfully all the time. Nothing dangerous, nothing cruel. Just help.

The drop fell before Raisa had consciously decided to tilt her wrist. It caught the light as it descended, impossibly green, and landed on the cookie's rough oatmeal surface where it spread slightly, darkening the beige to brown in a small circle no bigger than a pencil eraser.

There. Done.

Raisa set the vial down and picked up a clean spoon, using its back to spread the drop across more of the cookie's surface, working the liquid into the textured ridges. Within seconds, no visible trace remained. Just an ordinary oatmeal raisin cookie, indistinguishable from its companions except that Raisa knew exactly which one it was.

Her hands weren't shaking. That surprised her slightly. She'd expected some physical manifestation of having crossed a line she'd known better than to cross. But her fingers remained steady as she arranged the cookies on the plate, positioned the marked one slightly forward, carried everything to the patio table where Kenz was already bouncing in her seat.

"Oh good, oatmeal raisin, I actually really like these even though everyone says they're the boring cookie, but I think raisins are underrated, they're like little sweet explosions, and the oatmeal has that chewy texture." Kenz reached for the nearest cookie, which was not the one Raisa had prepared.

"Take this one," Raisa said, nudging the marked cookie forward with the edge of the plate. "It's the freshest."

"Okay!" Kenz grabbed it without suspicion, without hesitation, because why would she question her grandmother offering her a cookie? Why would an eleven-year-old child imagine that the person she trusted most in the world had just administered something without her knowledge or consent?

Raisa sat down across from her and watched Kenz devour the cookie in approximately four bites, barely pausing in her stream-of-consciousness narration about the garden, about whether the earthworms they'd disturbed could actually hear approaching footsteps or just felt vibrations, about how she'd counted seventeen dandelions in the weedy section but there might have been more because she'd lost track when that beetle appeared again.

The cookie was gone. Kenz reached for the lemonade, drained half the glass in one long swallow, set it down and immediately picked up another cookie, one of the unmarked ones, and kept talking, kept moving, her whole body involved in every sentence.

Done. Whatever was going to happen was now irreversible. Raisa felt something settle in mind that wasn't quite relief and wasn't quite guilt but lived somewhere in the uncomfortable territory between them.

"How do you feel?" she asked, then immediately regretted the question's transparency.

But Kenz just grinned, crumbs at the corner of her mouth. "Good! Hungry, I guess I worked up an appetite, and my knees are a little sore from kneeling but that's okay, and I'm excited to get back to the garden, I was thinking maybe I could help with the actual dividing part this time, not just the weeding, I promise I'll be really careful."

"We'll see," Raisa said. "Why don't you finish your snack first."

She watched Kenz consume the remaining cookies and lemonade with undiminished enthusiasm, watched her granddaughter's hands gesture through the air as she talked, watched the constant motion of bouncing knee and tapping fingers and slight rocking in the chair that meant some part of Kenz was always, always moving.

When would it start working? Elizabeth hadn't specified a timeline, but surely something plant-based and meant to calm nervous energy would take effect relatively quickly. Ten minutes? Twenty?

Kenz pushed back from the table. "Okay, I'm ready to get back to work! Should I finish the weeding in that other bed, or do you want me to start on something else, or—Oh, look, there's a bird in the rosebush. Is that a finch? I think it might be a finch. We studied birds in science class and--"

"Go back to the weeding," Raisa said, hearing the tightness in her own voice. "I'll be out in a few minutes to check on you."

She stayed at the patio table after Kenz bounced away, energy utterly unchanged, chaos undiminished. She watched the girl drop to her knees in the garden bed and immediately start pulling plants with the same unfocused enthusiasm that had characterized the entire morning.

It hadn't worked.

Or it hadn't worked yet.

She gathered the empty plate and glass and brought them inside, moving through the familiar motions of rinsing and loading the dishwasher while her mind spun. How long should she wait? What if the potion was too subtle to notice at first? What if the change were gradual rather than immediate? Elizabeth had described it as gentle, as working with the body's natural rhythms. Perhaps that meant a slow onset rather than a dramatic shift.

She placed the vial back in the bathroom cabinet, tucking it behind the vitamin bottles again. Then she stood in front of the mirror and studied her own face. It looked competent and controlled, showing no sign of the transgression she'd just committed or the doubt beginning to curl through her certainty.

Outside the bathroom window, she could see a corner of the garden where Kenz worked, her small figure bent over the perennial bed, hands moving in constant motion.

Give it time. Be patient. It would work. It had to work, because if it didn't, she had violated Elizabeth's explicit instructions and her granddaughter's autonomy for nothing.

She returned to the kitchen and occupied herself with unnecessary tasks: wiping already-clean counters, reorganizing the spice cabinet, anything to keep her hands busy while time passed. The kitchen clock ticked steadily. Five minutes became ten, which became fifteen.

Through the window, Kenz continued her enthusiastic assault on the garden beds, apparently experiencing no calming effects whatsoever.

Maybe the dosage had been too conservative. Elizabeth had said one drop, but what if Kenz's particular energy level required more? What if—

No. She cut off that line of thinking immediately. Elizabeth had been explicit about the dosage, and Raisa had already ignored the more important instruction about consent. She would not compound the violation by exceeding the recommended amount.

Twenty minutes. Thirty. The clock's hands moved with their customary precision, while her anxiety built with a less predictable rhythm.

She should check on the garden progress. That was reasonable, wasn't it? A grandmother checking on her granddaughter's work. Nothing unusual about that. And if Kenz seemed calmer, more focused, if the potion had finally taken effect, then she could stop this anxious watching and simply enjoy the afternoon the way she'd hoped.

She stepped out onto the patio and walked toward the perennial beds. Kenz was in the far section now, the area where she had been planning to divide the black-eyed Susans. Her granddaughter's back was to her, bent over in that characteristic pose of intense but unfocused engagement, hands pulling something from the ground with typical Kenz-like vigor.

And beside her, perhaps six feet away in the adjacent bed, another figure worked with identical energy, identical posture, and identical strawberry blonde hair.

Raisa stopped walking.

Her brain tried several explanations in rapid succession: one of the neighborhood children had wandered over; Kenz had called a friend without asking permission; someone had arrived while she was inside and Kenz, being Kenz, had immediately recruited them to help.

The second figure straightened up, arms full of pulled plants, and turned slightly. Raisa saw her face in profile.

Kenz's face minus Kenz's glasses. Kenz's grass-stained jeans and striped t-shirt, and the same smudge of dirt on her left cheek that had been there all afternoon.

Impossible.

Raisa's vision blurred briefly, and she blinked hard, certain she was seeing double, that stress or exhaustion or guilt had finally broken something in her visual processing. She'd heard of such things: fatigue causing optical illusions, the mind conjuring what couldn't be real.

She closed her eyes. Counted to three. Opened them.

Both figures were still there, both working with enthusiastic chaos in the garden beds. Both completely, impossibly real.

The one wearing glasses, the original, Raisa's mind supplied frantically, because one of them had to be original, looked up and caught sight of her.

"Grandma! Come see, I've been working on the black-eyed Susans, well, we've been working on them, and I think I'm getting better at telling what should stay and what should go, except there was this one plant that I wasn't totally sure about so I left it, and... oh, are you okay? You look kind of pale. Do you need to sit down?"

The concern in Kenz's voice was genuine and completely characteristic. The girl, for all her chaos, had always been acutely attuned to other people's distress. It was one thing she loved about her, that underneath the whirlwind of energy lived a deeply empathetic child who noticed when people were struggling.

"I'm fine," she heard herself say, though her voice sounded distant and strange to her own ears. "I just—who—"

The second figure straightened up at the sound of Raisa's voice and turned fully toward her. Same face. Same smile. Same grass-stained knees and untucked t-shirt. The only difference Raisa could discern was that this one wasn't wearing glasses.

"Hi, Grandma!" the second Kenz said with equal enthusiasm and equal affection. "We're making really good progress! I think we've almost cleared this whole section, and I only pulled one thing I shouldn't have, but I caught it right away and put it back, so that's improvement, right?"

We. She'd said we.

Raisa's mind, which prided itself on practical problem-solving and logical analysis, simply refused to process what her eyes were reporting. This couldn't be happening. People didn't duplicate. Eleven-year-old girls didn't suddenly become plural. Reality didn't work that way.

Except she was looking at two Kenzes, both of whom seemed utterly unconcerned about the existence of the other, both of whom were behaving exactly as Kenz always behaved: enthusiastic, chaotic, well-meaning, and completely oblivious to the fact that anything unusual was occurring.

The vial. The drop on the cookie. Elizabeth's warning about the potion working with the body's natural rhythms, not against them.

Oh God. Oh God, what had she done?

"Grandma?" The original Kenz, the one with glasses, was walking toward her now, face creased with worry. "Seriously, you don't look good. Do you want some water? Should I call Mom?"

"No," she said sharply, then softened her tone with an effort that felt like lifting stones. "No, don't call your mother. I'm just—I need a moment. You two—" The word felt impossible in her mouth. "You two keep working. I'll be right back."

She turned and walked toward the house with measured steps that wanted to become a run. Her mind was racing now, trying to understand, to find the logical explanation that would make this make sense.

Magic. It had to be magic, actual impossible magic, not just herbal compounds and traditional knowledge but something that could bend reality itself. Elizabeth had given her something that could duplicate a human being, that could take one chaotic eleven-year-old and create a second equally real version, and Raisa had administered it without consent, without understanding, with no conception of what it might actually do.

Inside the house, she gripped the edge of the kitchen sink and stared at her white knuckles. Through the window, she could see both girls working in the garden, moving in chaotic rhythm, pulling plants and chattering to each other with apparent ease.

Both of them were real. That was what paralyzed her thinking more than anything else. This wasn't an illusion, or a projection, or a hallucination. Both girls had solid bodies, cast shadows, and interacted with physical objects. Both were fully present, fully aware, fully Kenz.

Which meant what? That one was the original and one was... what? A copy? A duplicate? A magical construct? And how could Raisa possibly tell which was which when they both seemed equally alive, equally conscious, equally deserving of—

She cut off that thought before it could complete itself.

The practical problems assembled themselves in her mind with brutal efficiency: Claire was coming to pick up one Kenz in approximately two hours. What would Raisa say when there were two? How could she possibly explain this? She couldn't. Which meant she had to fix it before her daughter arrived.

But how did one fix impossible duplication? There was no logical framework for this, or step-by-step process to reverse magical mishaps.

Elizabeth. The thought arrived with the force of certainty. Elizabeth was the only person who might understand what had happened, the only person who knew about the potion and its properties, the only person who might hopefully, please God, know how to undo what Raisa had done, but Elizabeth lived on the Miller farm, a twenty-minute drive away. And Raisa couldn't leave two Kenzes unsupervised in her house for the hour it would take to drive there collect Elizabeth and get back. Kenz alone was overwhelming; two of her would be catastrophic.

She could bring them with her. Load both girls into the van and take them to the farm and explain to Elizabeth what had happened and beg for help to fix it before...

The kitchen clock showed 1:47. Claire would arrive at three. Seventy-three minutes to get to the Miller farm, explain the situation, find a solution, and reverse whatever impossible thing the potion had done.

Not enough time. Raisa felt panic trying to claw its way up her throat and forced it down through sheer will. Panic was useless. Panic solved nothing. She was a person who stayed calm in a crisis, who found solutions, who handled what needed handling. Except she'd never had to handle this kind of crisis before. Had never imagined needing to.

Through the window, both girls were still working in the garden, apparently content, apparently real, apparently permanent.

Raisa went to the bathroom cabinet and retrieved the vial. She studied the green liquid through the glass. How? How had one drop of this created an entire additional human being? What had Elizabeth given her that could do such a thing?

What had Raisa done to her granddaughter?

The guilt that had been sitting dormant in her stomach suddenly surged upward with nauseating force. She gripped the edge of the sink again, breathing carefully, refusing to give in to the physical manifestation of her mistake.

Fix it. That was all that mattered now. Not guilt, not panic, not the desperate wish to undo the last hour. Just the immediate practical necessity of figuring out how to reverse the duplication before her daughter arrived and discovered what she had done.

She pocketed the vial; evidence, and possibly necessary for Elizabeth to understand what had gone wrong, and she returned to the kitchen window. The Kenzes were sitting back on their heels now, apparently taking a break, talking to each other with animated hand gestures that mirrored each other like reflections.

Chapter 4

She stepped back out onto the patio. "Kenz," she called, then stopped, uncertain how to address them. "Girls, come inside," she called, hearing an edge creep into her voice and unable to smooth it away. "Right now, please."

"But we're making such good progress," the original Kenz protested, gesturing at the bed with muddy gloves that scattered soil across the grass. "Look how much we've cleared, and I think I'm finally getting the hang of which plants are which, well, mostly, there was that one hosta but I put it right back."

"Mackenzie." She used her granddaughter's full name, the tone she reserved for non-negotiable moments. "Inside. Now."

The firmness in her voice finally penetrated. Both girls scrambled to their feet with identical graceless enthusiasm, identical grass stains on their knees, identical smudges of dirt across their identical faces. They followed her toward the house, chattering to each other about what they'd accomplished, their voices overlapping in a way that made her head throb.

In the kitchen, under the bright overhead light that suddenly felt harsh enough to expose every flaw in her understanding of reality, Raisa turned to face them both. They stood side by side, and the similarities were absolutely perfect. Same height, same build, same strawberry blonde hair. The only distinguishing feature was the glasses on one and the slight variation in the dirt patterns on their clothes that would disappear the moment they changed or washed.

"How do you feel?" Raisa asked, directing the question to both of them while studying their faces for any sign of distress or awareness that something was wrong.

"Good!" they answered in unison, then giggled at the synchronization. "Tired, maybe," the one with glasses added. "But good tired, like we've been doing real work, not just sitting around."

"And hungry," the other one chimed in. "I'm always hungry after working outside; all that fresh air makes you hungry. I wonder why that is? Maybe it's the extra oxygen or the physical activity increasing your metabolism."

"Do either of you notice anything unusual?" Raisa tried, though she could already see from their expressions that they didn't. They were too absorbed in their own experience, their attention already fragmented toward other things. The one without glasses was examining the magnetic letters on Raisa's refrigerator, rearranging them into words while she talked. The one with glasses had noticed a spider in the ceiling's corner and was tracking its movements with fascinated focus.

"Unusual how?" one of them asked, though Raisa had already lost track of which one had spoken. "Like unusual weather, unusual, or unusual like something weird happened unusual, because that spider is actually really cool. Look at how it's building that web; the pattern is almost geometric."

She pressed her fingers against her temples where the headache was building into something that felt like it might split her skull. They didn't know. Somehow, impossibly, neither of them had any awareness that there were now two of them. They were just... Kenz. Being Kenz. Existing in duplicate without any consciousness that reality had fundamentally broken.

She needed Elizabeth. Elizabeth understood the potion, understood herbs and their properties, and how magic worked in this world that she clearly didn't. Elizabeth could explain this, could fix this, could restore reality to its proper configuration before—

Before what? Before her Claire arrived to pick Kenz up and found two identical children? Before the neighbors noticed? Before the impossible situation spiraled even further beyond her control?

The vial was still in her pocket. She pulled it out with shaking hands that finally betrayed the panic she'd been holding beneath her careful composure. The green liquid inside looked exactly as it had this morning: harmless, plant-based, and safe. Elizabeth had said it was safe.

But Elizabeth had also said consent mattered. She had explicitly instructed Raisa to tell Kenz what she was giving her. And Raisa had ignored that instruction, had administered the drop secretly, had treated her granddaughter's autonomy as less important than her own need for a manageable afternoon.

This was her fault. This impossible disaster directly resulted from her arrogance, her desperation, her certainty that she knew better than the herbalist who had been working with these compounds for decades.

"Grandma?" The original Kenz, the one with glasses, Raisa's mind insisted on the distinction even though it might be meaningless, was looking at her with concern now, the spider forgotten. "You really don't look good. Should I call Mom?"

"No." The word came out sharper than she intended. She took a breath, tried again. "No, don't call your mother. I just... I need to make a phone call. I need you both to stay here in the kitchen. Don't touch anything. Don't go outside. Just sit down at the table and stay there until I come back."

She didn't wait to see if they obeyed. Her phone was in her purse in the living room, and she moved toward it with the single-minded focus of someone clinging to the only action that made sense. Call Elizabeth. Explain what happened. Get instructions for fixing this before it got worse.

Her fingers trembled as she scrolled through her contacts to Elizabeth's number. Pressed call. Listened to it ring once, twice, three times before she remembered with sinking certainty: the Amish didn't have phones in their homes. Elizabeth might have a phone in the barn for business calls, but she wouldn't be monitoring it on a Saturday afternoon. The chances of her answering were—

Voicemail. Elizabeth's calm voice asking callers to leave a message and promising to return calls within a day or two.

A day or two. Her daughter, Claire, would arrive in less than two hours.

She ended the call without leaving a message and stood in her living room, phone clutched in her hand, while her competence, the thing she'd built her entire identity around, crumbled. She couldn't fix this alone, couldn't manage it, couldn't control it, couldn't solve it through careful planning and execution. She needed help, and the person who could help wasn't reachable by phone.

She had to drive to the Miller farm in person, which meant leaving two Kenzes unsupervised in her house for the twenty minutes it would take to get there.

From the kitchen came the sound of chairs scraping, voices overlapping in an excited discussion of something, and the refrigerator opening. Raisa closed her eyes. They'd lasted approximately ninety seconds following her instructions to stay seated and not touch anything.

She returned to find both girls making sandwiches with the unsystematic enthusiasm they brought to everything. Peanut butter on one counter, jelly on another, bread pulled from the bag and stacked haphazardly, knives left sticky on the cutting board. One Kenz was eating directly from the jar of peanut butter while the other spread jelly with enough force to tear through the bread.

"I told you to sit at the table," Raisa said, hearing the futility in her own voice even as she spoke.

"We were hungry," one Kenz said around a mouthful of peanut butter. "And you were gone for a while, well, not a while while, but we didn't know when you'd be back, and my stomach was growling, did you hear it? It was so loud."

"We made you a sandwich too," the other one added helpfully, holding up a creation that looked like it contained more jelly than bread and had been assembled without any attention to whether the edges aligned. "You should eat something. You look really pale still; maybe you're dehydrated. That's what Mom always says when I get that weird pale look."

Raisa took the sandwich because it was easier than arguing. Set it carefully on the counter because eating was impossible when her stomach felt like it had been replaced with concrete. "Thank you," she managed. "That was thoughtful."

Their identical faces lit up with identical pleasure at the praise. They were trying to help, both of them - however many there actually were - genuinely wanted to take care of her, to make things better. They just did not know that their existence was the crisis, that their less than carefully made sandwich couldn't solve the problem of their impossible duplication.

"I need to go out for a little while," Raisa said, choosing her words carefully. "I need you both to stay here, in the house. Do not go outside. Do not answer the door if anyone knocks. Do not call your mother or anyone else. Just stay here and..." What could she tell them to do that would actually occupy their attention for three-quarters of an hour? "You can watch television. There are snacks in the pantry. Just please, please stay inside."

"Where are you going?" they asked in unison, then giggled at the synchronization again.

"I need to visit Mrs. Miller. It's important. I won't be gone long, but I need you to promise me you'll follow the rules. Stay inside. Don't answer the door. Don't call anyone. Can you promise me that?"

Both nodded with identical earnestness, identical intention to comply that she knew from experience would last approximately until something more interesting caught their attention. But she had no choice. Elizabeth was the only person who might understand what had happened, who might know how to reverse it, who could explain why a simple herbal calming compound had somehow duplicated a human being.

She got them settled in the living room with the television turned to some nature documentary about coral reefs that briefly captured their attention and put a bowl of pretzels on the coffee table. She stood in the doorway, watching them for a moment, trying to memorize which was which even though she knew it was futile. The one with glasses sat on the left side of the couch. The one without glasses had already gotten up to examine a photograph on the bookshelf, her attention hooked by something in the image's background.

"Remember," she said, "stay inside. Don't answer the door. I'll be back soon."

"Okay, Grandma," they chorused, their attention already fragmenting between the television, the pretzels, the photograph, the texture of the couch cushions.

Raisa grabbed her purse and keys and left her house before she could second-guess the decision. Before she could fully acknowledge that she was abandoning two eleven-year-old children, or one eleven-year-old child duplicated unsupervised in her home while she drove nearly an 45 minutes round trip for help she wasn't even certain Elizabeth could provide.

The van felt like a refuge. Her hands knew what to do here: turn the key, check the mirrors, back out of the driveway with the careful precision she'd maintained for decades of driving. She could see her living room window from the street, could make out two small figures on the couch, still apparently watching television. Still apparently following instructions.

She knew better than to trust that. Kenz's intentions were always good. Her follow-through was what failed, her attention scattering the moment something more interesting appeared. Within five minutes, they'd be up and moving. Within ten, they might be back outside or rummaging through Raisa's things or calling her daughter to report that Grandma had left them alone.

Raisa's foot pressed harder on the accelerator than it should have. She forced herself to release the tension, to drive the speed limit, to breathe in the measured way she'd learned decades ago when Claire was a colicky infant and she had thought she was drowning in exhaustion and responsibility.

The route to the Miller farm was familiar enough that she could drive it without conscious thought, which was fortunate because her mind refused to focus on the road. Instead, it kept circling back to the impossible scene in her garden; two Kenzes, both absolutely real, both utterly unaware that they shouldn't exist.

She'd crossed a line. That knowledge sat in her chest like a stone. Elizabeth had given explicit instructions: one drop, and make sure Kenz knew what she was receiving. Consent matters. And Raisa had heard those instructions and chosen – chosen - to ignore the second part. She had decided that her need to control the afternoon, to make Kenz manageable, was more important than her granddaughter's right to know what was being administered to her.

That decision had consequences. Standing in her garden looking at two identical children was the physical manifestation of her violation, reality itself reflecting back the wrongness of what she'd done.

Except the Kenzes didn't seem wrong. That was what made this harder than if they'd been obviously flawed or incomplete. Both girls were perfectly, completely Kenz. Same energy, same enthusiasm, same inability to sit still or focus or follow through on instructions. Same empathy that noticed when Raisa looked pale and offered worried suggestions about water and shade. Same loving granddaughter, duplicated.

It all raised questions she could not consider right now but knew would have to be addressed eventually: if both were real, both conscious, both fully present... what happened if Elizabeth could reverse this? Would they be destroying a person? Would one cease to exist? And who decided which one counted as the original, the one with rights to continued existence?

Her knuckles had gone white on the steering wheel again. She forcibly relaxed her grip, flexed her fingers, tried to push those thoughts away. First things first: get to Elizabeth. Explain what happened. Find out if reversal was even possible.

Deal with the philosophical implications later.

The familiar landmarks rolled past her windows. The Beiler farm where laundry had been on the lines this morning. The Fisher place where the youngest boy had waved from his fence. The turn onto Miller Road, the gravel drive that led to the white farmhouse and the red barn where Elizabeth would be finishing afternoon chores, preparing dinner, settling into the evening routine of a farm family.

She pulled into the drive and turned off the engine then sat for a moment in the sudden silence, gathering herself. Her reflection in the rearview mirror showed a woman who looked every one of her sixty-seven years and then some. The lines around her mouth seemed deeper than they'd been this morning, and the shadows under her eyes spoke of stress her careful composure couldn't quite hide.

She looked like someone who'd made a terrible mistake and was desperately hoping someone else could fix it.

Which was exactly what she was.

She climbed out of the van and walked toward the farmhouse, each step feeling heavier than the last. Twenty minutes away, two identical granddaughters were probably already ignoring her instructions, already creating new chaos, already proving that her attempt to control them had failed as completely as everything else she'd tried today.

Elizabeth answered the door at Raisa's knock, and her warm smile faded immediately to concern. "Raisa? What's wrong? You look—"

"I need your help," Raisa interrupted, hearing the rawness in her own voice. "The potion. The one you gave me. I used it, and something went wrong. Something impossible."

Elizabeth's eyes went to the vial Raisa had pulled from her pocket, still more than half full of green liquid, and her expression shifted into something Raisa couldn't quite read. Not anger. Not judgment. Something closer to careful assessment, the way Elizabeth looked at a plant she was trying to diagnose.

"Come inside," Elizabeth said quietly. " Come inside. Tell me exactly what happened."

Chapter 5

The kitchen smelled like it always did: bread baking, herbs drying, and the scent that came from a wood-burning stove that had been tended since morning.

One corner of the long wooden table was still scattered with the remnants of afternoon work. Elizabeth's journal lay open beside several small jars, a measuring spoon, pages filled with her careful handwriting documenting some experiment or observation.

Samuel stood at the far end of the kitchen, preparing to head out for evening chores. He nodded at Raisa, his weathered face showing mild surprise at this unexpected visit, but not alarm. Elizabeth must have communicated something with a glance or gesture Raisa missed, because Samuel simply collected his hat from its peg and headed toward the door.

"I'll start the milking," he said quietly, his hand pausing briefly on Elizabeth's shoulder as he passed. It was a slight gesture that carried volumes: support, trust, and the assurance that he'd manage whatever needed managing while she dealt with whatever crisis had brought Raisa here looking like her world had ended.

The door closed behind him with a soft click.

"Sit," Elizabeth said, pulling out a chair at the table and nudging her herbs aside to make room. "You look ready to collapse."

She sat because her knees agreed with Elizabeth's assessment. Her hands found the table's worn surface, and her fingers traced old stains and gouges that spoke of decades of use. This table had seen countless family meals, children's lessons, and Elizabeth's herb work. It had absorbed the overflow of a full life lived in service and faith and the kind of love that showed itself through action.

Raisa had violated all of those things. She had taken Elizabeth's carefully offered help and twisted it into deception, had imposed her will on a child who trusted her, had shattered some fundamental truth about how reality should work.

"The potion," she started, then found her throat had closed around the words. She pulled the vial from her pocket again and set it on the table between them like an accusation. "I gave it to Kenz. This morning. Without telling her. Without her consent."

Elizabeth's eyes went to the vial with its impossible green liquid and her expression shifted into something Raisa couldn't quite read. Not anger, though Raisa would have understood anger. Something closer to the look she got when examining a patient with unexpected symptoms, that analytical focus that wanted to understand before judging.

"And?" Elizabeth's voice remained level, gentle even, though Raisa could hear the tension underneath. "What happened?"

This was the part that would sound insane. The part where Raisa would say words that made no sense and watch Elizabeth's face change from concern to disbelief to the careful politeness people used when dealing with someone who'd clearly lost their grip on reality.

"It duplicated her," Raisa said, the words coming out flat and factual because any other tone would shatter what remained of her composure.

"One drop on a cookie, just like you said. She ate it. And twenty minutes later there were two of them. Two Kenzes, both completely real, both working in my garden like nothing was wrong, both absolutely convinced they were the original."

The silence that followed felt like it lasted for years. Elizabeth sat very still, her hands folded on the table in front of her, her attention fixed on Raisa's face with an intensity that made Raisa want to look away. But she held that gaze, because if she was going to confess this impossible disaster, she owed Elizabeth the courage to face her reaction directly.

"Two," Elizabeth repeated finally, the word barely above a whisper. "You're certain?"

"I was looking right at them. Both solid, both talking, both..." Raisa's hands moved helplessly, trying to gesture toward an impossibility that had no shape. "Both absolutely, completely real. I left them at my house. Watching television. Unsupervised. Because I had to get here, had to find you, had to—" Her voice cracked. "Elizabeth, I don't know what I've done. I don't know how to fix it."

The admission cost more than Raisa had expected. She was the person who fixed things, who solved problems, who maintained control even when circumstances spun beyond anyone's reasonable management. Saying out loud that she was helpless, that she needed rescue, that her vaunted competence had failed completely felt like admitting a kind of death.

Elizabeth stood abruptly and moved to the shelves that lined one wall of the kitchen, her fingers already reaching for the thick leather journal, the binding worn soft from generations of handling, pages filled with handwriting in multiple styles as knowledge passed from woman to woman. Elizabeth brought it back to the table with the reverent focus she'd give to a medical emergency, already flipping through pages covered in cramped notations.

"Duplication," she murmured, more to herself than to Raisa. "I've never - in thirty years of working with these compounds - I've never heard of anything like that." Her fingers traced down a page, then flipped forward, backward, searching for something that might explain the impossible.

"You said it was safe," Raisa heard herself say, and hated the accusation in her voice even as she couldn't call it back. "You said at worst it would do nothing."

"For the uses I've made of it, that's true." Elizabeth didn't look up from the journal, but her voice had sharpened slightly. "Did you do exactly as I instructed? One drop, mixed into food or drink?"

"Yes. One drop on an oatmeal cookie. I watched her eat it."

"And you told her what you were giving her? You explained, got her consent?"

The question landed like a stone in Raisa's stomach. She wanted to lie, wanted to claim she'd followed every instruction perfectly, wanted to make this anyone's fault but her own. But Elizabeth deserved better. Kenz deserved better.

"No," Raisa said quietly. "I didn't tell her. I... I put it on the cookie and made sure she ate that specific one and said nothing. I knew you'd told me consent mattered. I heard you say it, but I... I thought that was just... I didn't think it was essential to how it worked. I thought you meant ethically, not practically."

Elizabeth's hands stilled on the journal pages. She looked up, and Raisa saw something in her face that was harder than disappointment, sharper than disapproval. It was the look of a practitioner confronting misuse of her craft, of someone whose carefully maintained boundaries had been violated.

"Everything I do is both," Elizabeth said, her voice carrying an edge Raisa had never heard before. "Ethics and practice aren't separate in this work. The consent isn't decorative, Raisa. It's foundational. The body responds differently to what it accepts versus what's imposed. The mind matters. The will matters."

"I know," Raisa said, which was inadequate but true. "I knew when I did it. I just... I was desperate, and I thought I could manage one small compromise if it meant getting through the afternoon without more destruction."

"And now?" Elizabeth's question wasn't cruel, but it was firm. "Was it worth it?"

Raisa thought of two Kenzes in her living room, both real, both her granddaughter, both existing because she'd decided her need for control mattered more than a child's autonomy. She thought of Claire scheduled to arrive in - she glanced at the clock on Elizabeth's wall - less than ninety minutes now, expecting to collect one daughter and finding the impossible instead.

"No," she whispered. "God, no, it wasn't worth it."

Something in Elizabeth's posture softened slightly. She returned her attention to the journal, flipping pages with renewed purpose. "Tell me everything. Exact timeline. When did she consume it? When did you first notice the duplication? Describe exactly what you saw."

Raisa walked through it step by step, giving the cookie at approximately 12:30, checking on Kenz around 1:00 and finding her unchanged, returning to the garden at 1:20 and seeing two figures working in separate beds. Elizabeth listened with the focused attention of a diagnostician, occasionally asking clarifying questions: Had the duplication been instantaneous or gradual? Were both Kenzes aware of each other? Did they show any distress or confusion? Had Raisa noticed any pattern to their behavior?

"They acted exactly like Kenz always acts," she explained, hearing the helplessness in her voice. "Both of them. Same energy, same enthusiasm, same inability to sit still or follow instructions for more than thirty seconds. They giggled when they spoke in unison, like it was a game. Neither seemed to understand that anything unusual had happened."

Elizabeth had pulled a blank page toward herself and was taking notes now, her handwriting quick and precise. "The potion works with the body's natural rhythms," she said, speaking slowly as if thinking through the problem out loud. "It's designed to support and enhance, never to suppress or force. With adults suffering from anxiety or restlessness, it helps their system find its own calm, channeling nervous energy into productive focus."

"But Kenz isn't anxious," Raisa said, understanding dawning cold in her chest. "She has ADHD. Her energy isn't nervous; it's expansive. It's how her brain is wired."

"Exactly." Elizabeth tapped her pen against the page, leaving small dots of ink that might have been unconscious punctuation or might have been the physical manifestation of her thinking. "So, when you gave her something designed to work with energy rather than against it, to enhance and channel rather than suppress..."

"It gave her more," Raisa finished. "It literalized her expansiveness. Made it physical."

"That's my theory." Elizabeth's voice carried the uncertainty of someone working at the edge of her knowledge. "Though, I've never seen or heard of anything like this in all my years of practice, in all my grandmother's records, in any of the texts I've studied. This is unprecedented."

The word should have been terrifying, but instead Raisa found it oddly comforting. At least she hadn't simply failed to implement a standard procedure correctly. She'd stumbled into territory no one had mapped before.

"Can you reverse it?" The question came out more plea than inquiry. "Is there a way to... undo the duplication? To get back to just one Kenz?"

Elizabeth was quiet for a long moment, her attention seemingly on the journal though Raisa suspected she was seeing something beyond the page. When she spoke, her voice carried the weight of her faith in a way Raisa had heard before, a seriousness that came from beliefs held deeply enough to shape every decision.

"That depends," Elizabeth said carefully, "on what exactly has been created. If the second Kenz is simply a magical construct, an illusion given temporary substance, then yes, withdrawing the magic should dissolve the duplication. But if she's actually been... brought into being as a separate entity, with her own consciousness, her own soul..."

She trailed off, and Raisa felt something cold settle in her stomach.

"You're asking if she's a person," Raisa said flatly. "If both of them are equally real, equally deserving of existence."

"I'm asking what happens when we try to reverse this," Elizabeth said. "Because if both Kenzes are fully present, fully conscious, fully themselves, and from what you've described, they seem to be, then 'reversing' the duplication might not be restoration. It might be... something else."

The word Elizabeth wasn't saying hung in the kitchen air between them: death, or erasure, or some other sort of metaphysical violence Raisa didn't have language for but could feel the shape of, heavy and terrible.

"I can't—" Raisa started, then stopped, because she didn't know how to finish that sentence. She couldn't leave two Kenzes existing? She couldn't erase one of them? She couldn't explain any of this to her daughter? All true, all impossible, all competing for urgency in her spinning thoughts.

"We'll take this one step at a time," Elizabeth said, her voice gentle again, the practitioner's calm reasserting itself. "First, I need to get to your house and assess the situation directly. See both girls, observe how they're interacting, determine if there are any signs of instability or progression. Then we can start working on solutions."

She stood and began moving around the kitchen with swift efficiency, gathering items from her shelves and workspace. Small jars of dried herbs, a mortar and pestle, a collection of empty vials, measuring implements, her working journal. Each item was selected with clear purpose and packed into a canvas bag that looked like it had been assembled for exactly this kind of emergency.

"Will they keep duplicating?" Raisa asked, the thought arriving with fresh horror. "If the potion is still working in her system, could there be three by now? Four?"

"I don't know," Elizabeth admitted, which was both terrifying and reassuring in its honesty. "The dose was small, a drop, and Kenz's body has been processing it for hours now. If duplication was going to cascade, it likely would have started already. But we won't know for certain until we see her. Them."

She paused in her gathering, one hand still reaching for a jar on the high shelf, and turned to look at Raisa fully. "You understand this will be complicated," she said. "Not just the magical mechanics, but the ethical questions. My faith teaches me that every soul is precious, that personhood isn't something we can simply unmake for convenience. If both Kenzes are truly themselves..."

"I know," Raisa interrupted, because she couldn't hear the rest of that thought completed. "I know. But my daughter arrives in an hour and fifteen minutes expecting to pick up one child. She can't... I can't explain this. No one can know."

"Someone will have to know eventually," Elizabeth said gently. "If we can't reverse this quickly, if it turns out both girls are permanent--"

"Then I'll deal with that when it becomes inevitable," Raisa said, hearing the edge return to her voice. "Right now, I need you to help me understand what I've created and how to fix it before my family discovers what I've done."

Elizabeth studied her for a moment longer, then simply nodded and returned to her packing. She added her grandmother's journal to the bag last, treating the old leather binding with reverence even in her hurry.

"I'll leave a note for Samuel," she said, moving to the small desk in the corner where the family kept paper and pens for correspondence. "He'll need to know I've gone with you and might not be back before dark."

Raisa watched her write with quick, economical strokes, then fold the paper and leave it prominently on the kitchen table weighted down with a coffee mug. The simple domesticity of it; leaving a note for her husband before rushing off to deal with an impossible magical crisis, would have been funny if Raisa had any capacity left for humor.

"Ready?" Elizabeth asked, hefting her canvas bag and looking at Raisa with a calm focus that suggested she was already planning her approach, already thinking three steps ahead to assessment and intervention and the careful observation that would guide their next moves.

Raisa stood, her legs shakier than she wanted them to be, and nodded. "Thank you," she managed. "For not— for just—"

"We'll talk about what you did later," Elizabeth said, not unkindly but firmly. "Right now, we need to make sure Kenz is safe. Both of them."

They walked to the van together. Elizabeth settled into the passenger seat with her canvas bag on her lap, already opening the journal to a page marked with a pressed leaf. "Tell me more about Kenz's typical behavior," she said as Raisa backed out of the drive. "Her energy levels, her focus patterns, how she responds to structure and instruction."

They talked through the twenty-minute drive, Elizabeth asking questions with clinical precision while Raisa answered as honestly as she could manage. What medications was Kenz on? What were her sleep patterns like? Had she shown any adverse reactions to the cookie besides the duplication like nausea, dizziness, changes in energy?

The questions helped. They gave Raisa's mind something concrete to work with, a framework that felt almost normal even while discussing the profoundly abnormal. This was what she was good at; details, precision, careful observation and reporting.

Her phone sat silent in the cup holder between them. No calls from neighbors. No frantic messages from Claire asking why Kenz wasn't answering texts. No alerts from the police about disturbances involving identical children. She didn't know if the silence was a good sign or a terrifying one.

"What are you hoping we find when we arrive?" Elizabeth asked quietly as they merged onto the highway.

Raisa thought about that. In her most optimistic imagination: one Kenz, the duplication having dissolved naturally, her granddaughter watching television exactly where she'd been left. In her most realistic assessment: two Kenzes, both still blissfully unaware anything was wrong, probably having ignored every instruction and gotten into some new chaos.

"I'm hoping they're safe," she said finally. "Both of them. Whatever both means."

Elizabeth nodded, her attention returning to the journal in her lap, making additional notes in margins already crowded with generations of accumulated knowledge. Raisa kept her eyes on the road and her hands steady on the wheel, driving with the careful precision she'd maintained for decades.

Behind them, the Miller farm receded into the gathering evening. Ahead, Raisa's house waited with its impossible occupants and its ticking clock counting down to Claire's arrival.

And between them sat the canvas bag full of herbs and tools and centuries of wisdom, carried by a woman who believed in both science and souls, who would help solve this crisis while insisting they grapple with questions Raisa desperately wanted to avoid.

Raisa pressed slightly harder on the accelerator, watching the speed limit, but not exceeding it, because getting pulled over right now would add complications nobody needed.

Nineteen more minutes. Then they'd know what remained to be fixed, and what might have already moved beyond fixing.

The vial sat in the cup holder, its green promise not fully spent, but its warning fully realized.

Raisa kept driving.

Chapter 6

The house was empty.

Raisa knew it the moment she turned her key in the lock, before the door swung open into silence that felt too large, too still. The television was off. The pretzel bowl sat abandoned on the coffee table, a few scattered crumbs the only evidence that anyone had been there.

"Kenz?" She called out anyway, because not calling would mean accepting what she already knew. "Mackenzie? I'm home."

Nothing. Not even the familiar sound of Kenz's voice carrying from another room, mid-sentence in whatever thought had captured her attention.

Elizabeth followed her inside, canvas bag still on her shoulder, and took in the empty room with a single sweeping glance. "Upstairs?" she suggested, though her tone suggested she didn't believe it either.

They searched anyway. Raisa moving through her house with mounting dread that felt like water rising, each empty room another inch toward drowning. Her bedroom: undisturbed. The guest room: vacant. The bathroom where she'd hidden the vial just this morning, a decision that felt like it belonged to a different lifetime: empty. Kenz's usual sleeping space when she stayed over, the small room Raisa had furnished with twin beds and cheerful curtains years ago: beds neatly made, no sign of recent occupation.

Back downstairs, Elizabeth was examining the kitchen. "They made more sandwiches," she observed, pointing to the counter where fresh evidence of Kenz's characteristic food preparation sprawled. A peanut butter jar with the lid askew, a jelly knife left sticky on the cutting board, the bread bag open with several slices pulled out and not used. "Recently, I'd say. This bread hasn't dried out yet."

Raisa's mind tried to calculate timelines, to apply logic to a situation that had already proven itself beyond logic's jurisdiction. She'd left perhaps forty-five minutes ago. Less than an hour, and they were gone.

"They might have gone back to the garden," she said, moving toward the sliding door that led to her backyard. But even as she spoke, she could see through the glass that the garden beds lay empty, tools abandoned exactly where she'd left them hours ago. There were no compact figures working among the perennials and no sound of Kenz's voice explaining something fascinating she'd just remembered about root systems or pollination.

"Neighbors?" Elizabeth suggested gently, and Raisa felt something in her chest constrict because that meant asking, meant admitting she'd lost track of her granddaughter, meant exposing the situation to outside observation when she'd been so desperate to keep it contained.

But there was no choice. She couldn't search the entire neighborhood alone, and every minute that passed was another minute the Kenzes were unsupervised and potentially multiplying again.

The thought arrived with cold clarity. What if two had become four while she'd been gone? What if they were still multiplying, geometric progression creating an impossible army of eleven-year-olds, each one as enthusiastically chaotic as the original?

She forced her spiraling thoughts into submission through sheer will. "I'll check with the Hendersons next door," she said, hearing her voice come out calm, a masterpiece of deception. "You take the other side."

The Hendersons' doorbell chimed with a cheerful electronic melody that felt obscene given the circumstances. Mrs. Henderson appeared after a moment, wiping flour from her hands onto an apron, her face shifting from pleasant surprise to mild concern when she registered Raisa's expression.

"Raisa? Is everything all right?"

"I'm looking for my granddaughter," Raisa said, and was proud of how normal it sounded, how much like a routine inquiry rather than barely controlled panic. "She was at my house this afternoon. She's eleven years old, strawberry blonde hair, glasses. I stepped out briefly and now I can't find her. Did you happen to see her leave?"

Mrs. Henderson's forehead creased in thought. "I saw some girls earlier, actually. Walking up the street together, heading toward the square. I assumed they were friends of yours visiting." She paused. "Come to think of it, they did look quite alike. Sisters, maybe?"

Something cold settled in Raisa's stomach. "How many girls?"

"Oh, I'm not sure I counted exactly. Three? Four? They were chattering away, seeming very excited about something." Mrs. Henderson smiled. "You know how kids are at that age. Everything's an adventure."

Four. They'd multiplied again. Two had somehow become four during the brief window she'd been gone, and now they were loose in the village, heading toward the square, completely unsupervised and unaware that they represented an impossible violation of reality's basic rules.

"Thank you," Raisa managed, already turning away. "That's very helpful."

She met Elizabeth back at the van, where her friend's expression told a similar story. "The Kowalskis saw them too," Elizabeth reported. "Said there was a group of girls who looked like they might be related, all talking at once, heading toward the village square about twenty minutes ago."

Twenty minutes. Raisa's mind tried to calculate how much chaos four Kenzes could create in twenty minutes loose in a small village and couldn't arrive at any scenario that wasn't catastrophic.

They got into the van without discussion, Raisa's hands finding the steering wheel and turning the key with automatic precision while her thoughts raced ahead. Village square. That's where children went when they had energy and enthusiasm and no supervision, the little park with its gazebo and benches, the community bulletin board, the shops that lined the square's perimeter. Safe enough, usually. But nothing about this situation was usual.

She drove too fast, checking herself twice when her speed crept above the limit, forcing herself to maintain control of at least this one thing. Elizabeth sat beside her in the passenger seat, hands folded calmly in her lap, her presence a steadying reminder that Raisa wasn't facing this alone even though it felt like drowning in deep water.

"When we find them," Elizabeth said quietly, "we'll need to get them somewhere private quickly. The farm is the best option to manage them, privacy to work on a solution."

"My daughter is expecting Kenz back this evening," Raisa heard herself say. The word *evening* felt like a wall she was already failing to hold up.

"We'll deal with that when we find them," Elizabeth said. "First things first."

The village square appeared ahead, and Raisa's heart sank at what she saw even before she'd fully processed the scene. There, in the open area near the gazebo where the township held community events, were four identical strawberry blonde girls in grass-stained jeans and untucked striped t-shirts, all moving with characteristic Kenz energy around a pile of cardboard boxes and folding tables. And standing in the middle of them, holding a clipboard and looking like someone who'd stumbled into a surrealist painting, was Martin Fletcher, the township's volunteer coordinator.

Raisa pulled into a parking space with hands that had started shaking. Up close, the scene was worse than she'd imagined. The four Kenzes were attempting to help Martin set up for tomorrow's farmer's market, or rather, each one was helping independently while talking continuously, their voices overlapping in ways that created a wall of sound that was unmistakably, devastatingly Kenz.

"—and then we could arrange the tables in a semi-circle, that would make it easier for people to browse, I saw that at a market once, well, I think it was a market, it might have been a craft fair, but anyway—"

"—these boxes are heavy, should they be this heavy? Maybe we should unpack them first and then move them, that would make more sense, or does it make more sense to move them and then unpack them—"

"—Mr. Fletcher, did you know that farmers' markets have been around since ancient times? I read about it, well, I started reading about it. There was this really interesting article about Roman markets—"

"—I can totally carry three chairs at once, watch, see, isn't that helpful? Oh wait, that one's slipping. I've got it. No, wait—"

Martin looked up at Raisa's approach with the expression of a man who'd been trying to apply standard logic to an impossible situation and was losing his grip on sanity. "Mrs. Hartman? These girls said they were Mackenzie Hartman and I... I'm very confused because they all... I mean, they all say they're—"

"Grandma!" four voices in delighted unison. Four identical faces lit up with genuine pleasure at seeing her. Four sets of grass-stained knees and untucked t-shirts turned toward her with synchronized enthusiasm.

Only one wore glasses.

Raisa focused on that detail like a drowning person focusing on a lifeline. The one with the glasses was the original. The other three - God, the other three - were duplicates created by her violation, by her desperate need for control manifesting as this impossible multiplication of the very chaos she'd been trying to suppress.

"Girls," she said, and her voice came out remarkably steady, "we need to go now."

"But we're helping Mr. Fletcher set up for the market," one of the non-glasses Kenzes protested. "We're being really useful, he said so. Didn't you say so, Mr. Fletcher? We've carried all these boxes and we're arranging the tables and—"

"I appreciated the offer," Martin said carefully, his eyes moving between the four identical girls with the confusion of someone whose understanding of reality was being actively challenged. "But I'm still not clear are you all related? Quadruplets? I've never seen—"

"Family situation," Elizabeth interjected smoothly, appearing at Raisa's elbow with the canvas bag still on her shoulder. "We're handling it. Thank you for your patience with them, Mr. Fletcher. We'll take them home now."

"But we're not done helping," the original Kenz said, Raisa could tell because the glasses caught the late-afternoon light. "We only got half the tables set up and Mr. Fletcher had all these chairs and we were going to arrange the vendor spaces and—"

"Now," Raisa said, and something in her tone finally penetrated. Four faces fell in identical expressions of disappointment, but they began moving toward the van with the dragging reluctance of children pulled away from something they'd been enjoying.

Getting four eleven-year-olds into a van designed for transporting Amish families to medical appointments proved more complicated than Raisa had anticipated. They all tried to get in at once, talking over each other about who should sit where, whether the windows could be opened, had Raisa seen how helpful they'd been with the market setup, and wasn't

Mr. Fletcher nice even though he seemed a little confused about something they couldn't quite figure out.

Raisa stood by the driver's door and watched Elizabeth herd them into the back seats with patient efficiency, redirecting energy and enthusiasm into the simple task of buckling seatbelts and settling into spaces.

Martin Fletcher approached as she opened the driver's door, his clipboard clutched like a shield. "Mrs. Hartman, I don't mean to pry, but should I reach out to the family again? I wasn't sure who to contact and the number I had on file—"

"I'll handle it," Raisa interrupted, more sharply than he deserved. "Thank you for your patience with the girls. I apologize for any confusion."

She got in before he could ask more. Elizabeth slid into the passenger seat, and Raisa turned the key with hands that had started trembling again.

The Miller farm. That was the only option now. Her house was too small, too exposed, too close to neighbors who'd already seen the girls. The farm had space, privacy, and a family who understood that some problems couldn't be solved through conventional means. Samuel would help. Elizabeth could work on a reversal in her kitchen while they figured out how to contain this disaster before it spread any further.

Behind her, the four Kenzes were already deep in conversation about the interesting work they'd done, how Mr. Fletcher had seemed confused about something they couldn't quite identify. Their voices blended and overlapped in ways that made it impossible to tell where one ended and another began, a chorus of Kenz that would have been funny if it wasn't so devastating.

"You need to call her," Elizabeth said quietly. "Before she calls the police."

Raisa's hands tightened on the steering wheel. "Not while I'm driving. Not until I know what I'm going to say."

Elizabeth didn't push. The October evening deepened around them as they drove. The familiar landmarks rolled past: the Beiler farm, the Fisher place, then the turn onto Miller Road. Real things. Normal things. The world continued its ordinary rotation while Raisa's personal reality had fractured into impossible pieces.

Chapter 7

The Miller farm appeared ahead through the van's windshield like a promise Raisa desperately wanted to believe in. The white farmhouse stood solid against the October evening sky, Everything was orderly and purposeful and anchored in rhythms that predated electricity. Behind her in the back seats, the four Kenzes maintained a constant stream of overlapping chatter that had transformed from individually manageable into a wall of sound, each voice indistinguishable from the others, building and building until Raisa's skull felt too small to contain it.

She pulled into the gravel drive with hands that ached from gripping the steering wheel too tightly for too long. She turned off the engine and let herself sit for just a moment in the sudden relative quiet. The Kenzes were still talking, but at least the van's motor had stopped adding to the noise.

Through the farmhouse windows she could see lamplight, warm and yellow in that way that came from actual flames rather than electricity. Amish homes had a quality of illumination she'd noticed over her fifteen years of driving for the community; softer somehow, more forgiving, the kind of light that didn't expose every flaw but instead suggested that flaws were simply part of being human and alive.

Elizabeth was already unbuckling her seatbelt, already reaching for the canvas bag of herbs and journals she'd assembled in what felt like another lifetime but had actually been less than an hour ago. "Ready?" she asked, and the gentleness in her voice made something in Raisa's chest constrict painfully.

She wasn't ready. Would never be ready to walk into Samuel Miller's home with four impossible children and ask for help managing a disaster of her own creation. But readiness had never been a requirement for doing what needed doing.

"Yes," Raisa said, and opened her door.

The evening air carried the scent of the farm to her immediately, earth and animals, the smell of worked land settling into evening rest, something green and growing from Elizabeth's extensive herb gardens. Beneath it all, the faint sweet smell of baked bread, because even in crisis, families still needed dinner. The normalcy of it felt like both comfort and accusation.

The van's side door slid open, and the four Kenzes tumbled out in an explosion of energy and enthusiasm that defied the late hour and the impossible circumstances of their existence. They hit the gravel drive already talking, already turning in circles to take in their surroundings, already firing questions into the evening air without waiting for answers.

"Is this the farm? The one with the chickens? Are the chickens still babies or are they bigger now? Can we see them? Are there other animals? What's that building? Is that the barn? It's so big, I didn't remember it being that big, or maybe I did but seeing it again makes it seem even bigger—"

"Do they have cows? I hear something that sounds like cows, or maybe that's not cows, what other animals make sounds like that? Oh, oh, look at the garden, Grandma, look how big their garden is, I bet they grow vegetables and herbs and—"

"Can we help with chores? I'm really good at chores, well, I'm trying to get better at chores, I can definitely carry things, I'm very strong for my age, my teacher said so, well, she said it about something else, but I think it applies to farm work too—"

"What's that smell? It smells like bread; is someone baking bread? I love bread, especially when it's fresh and still warm. Do you think we'll get to try some? Oh wow, look at the laundry on the line; those clothes are so different from—"

Raisa felt dizzy trying to track the four separate streams of consciousness, all overlapping, all authentically Kenz in their tangential enthusiasms and inability to complete a single thought before three others launched themselves into being. This was what she'd been trying to suppress with Elizabeth's potion, this relentless, exhausting, boundless energy that never paused, never settled, never allowed for quiet or order or the careful control Raisa had built her entire life around.

Look what that attempt had created instead.

The farmhouse door opened, and Samuel Miller emerged, backlit by the warm lamplight from within. He paused in the doorway for just a moment. Raisa saw him take in the scene with the same systematic assessment he probably brought to evaluating his fields or livestock. He took in the four small figures in the growing darkness, all identical, all in motion, all radiating the particular chaos that even one Kenz could generate.

His face showed surprise, but not shock. There was acceptance, not resignation. He was just a farmer confronting an unexpected situation that would require adaptation and work, approaching it the way he'd approach a fence that needed mending or a cow in difficult labor: steadily, pragmatically, with a faith that solutions existed if you were willing to put in the effort to find them.

He stepped out onto the porch, his solid frame somehow making the chaos in the driveway feel more manageable just by his presence. When he spoke, his voice carried the same calm authority Raisa had heard him use with his own children during the countless drives she'd provided over the years.

"Best bring them inside," Samuel said, looking directly at Raisa with eyes that held no judgment, only assessment. "We'll sort it out."

Four words. Just four words, but they landed in Raisa's chest like a benediction she hadn't known she needed. *We'll sort it out.* Not "you've created an impossible mess," not "how could you have done this," just the simple, pragmatic acknowledgment that a problem existed and would be addressed by people working together.

The Kenzes needed no encouragement. They surged toward the farmhouse with the enthusiasm they brought to everything, questions still flowing, hands already reaching to touch things: the porch railing, the doorframe, a hanging basket that had once held flowers but now showed only dried stems from the advancing season.

"Shoes," Samuel said, not loudly but with enough firmness that all four girls actually paused. "Off at the door. Line them up neat."

And they did it. All four of them dropped to the porch and began unlacing their sneakers with the kind of focused attention they'd failed to bring to anything in Raisa's garden. Something about Samuel's tone, or maybe just the novelty of a rule delivered without negotiation or explanation, had penetrated where Raisa's increasingly desperate instructions had bounced off like rain on waxed canvas.

Raisa followed them up the porch steps with Elizabeth beside her, watching four pairs of grass-stained sneakers line up in a crooked but genuine attempt at order. The sight made her throat tight. They were trying. They'd always been trying. That was the part she kept forgetting when the chaos mounted. Kenz wanted to help, wanted to please, wanted to do things right. She just couldn't, not consistently, not in the ways Raisa's rigid expectations demanded.

And now there were four of them, all trying and failing in perfect synchronization.

Inside, the farmhouse wrapped around Raisa like a worn quilt; familiar from years of picking Elizabeth up for appointments, but never experienced at quite this time of evening, never with quite this weight of crisis pressing down. The kitchen stretched along the back of the house, dominated by a long wooden table that showed decades of use in its stains and gouges and the particular shine that came from countless hands sliding across its surface. A wood stove radiated warmth from one corner, and yes, there was bread baking, the scent of it filling the air with a comfort so primal Raisa felt her shoulders drop slightly despite everything.

The four Kenzes spread through the kitchen like water finding its level, touching surfaces, examining jars on shelves, peering at the lamplight with fascination, asking questions about how you cooked without electricity and where did the bread smell come from and was that a butter churn and did they really use it or was it just decoration and—

"Girls." Samuel's voice, still not raised, still not harsh, cut through the noise like a warm knife through soft butter. "Hands to yourselves until you're invited to touch. Stand by the table."

They gravitated toward him, all that chaotic energy briefly contained by his steady presence. He looked at them for a long moment, and Raisa watched him count silently, his lips moving almost imperceptibly. One. Two. Three. Four. His eyebrows rose slightly—the closest thing to shock she'd seen from him yet.

"Four," he said, and it wasn't quite a question.

"Four," Elizabeth confirmed quietly, setting her canvas bag on the corner of the table where her herb work usually lived. "It's progressed since we left Raisa's house. There were two when she first called me."

Samuel nodded slowly, still studying the girls. His gaze moved across them systematically, and Raisa realized he was doing what she'd been doing compulsively since the first duplication, trying to find differences, trying to tell them apart, trying to determine which was the original.

Only one wore glasses. Her eyes went to that one automatically, seeking the anchor of familiarity. That one was Kenz, the real one, the original one, the one who'd arrived at Raisa's house this morning with such enthusiasm about helping in the garden. The others were... what? Copies? Duplicates? Complete separate individuals who happened to be identical?

The question made her head hurt.

"Can we see the chickens?" one of the non-glasses Kenzes asked, bouncing slightly on her bare feet. "We'll be really careful, we won't scare them, we're very good with animals usually, well, sometimes, there was this one time with a cat but that was different and—"

"Chores first," Samuel interrupted, not unkindly. "You want to help on a farm, you help with what needs doing, not just what sounds fun." He turned to Elizabeth. "You'll need your workspace for the potion work?"

Elizabeth nodded. "And quiet, if possible. This will take concentration."

"Then I'll take them out to the barn." Samuel's gaze moved to Raisa, and she saw the question in his eyes, the gentle offering of reprieve. "Your daughter?"

The words hit Raisa like cold water. Her daughter. Who Martin Fletcher had called hours ago now, who'd left increasingly frantic messages, who probably already thought something terrible had happened and was working herself into panic trying to reach Raisa and finding only silence.

Raisa pulled her phone from her pocket with hands that wanted to shake. The screen showed what she'd been avoiding looking at since they'd bundled the Kenzes out of the town square: seven missed calls. Four voicemails. Three text messages, each more urgent than the last.

The most recent: *Mom, I'm coming over. If I don't hear from you in the next hour I'm calling the police. What is going on with Kenz???*

Sent eighteen minutes ago.

"She knows something's wrong," Raisa heard herself say, her voice coming out flatter than she'd intended. "Martin called her. She's... she's probably on her way to my house right now."

"Then you need to call her," Samuel said, still gentle but with an edge of firmness that reminded Raisa he was a father of five, that managing crisis was part of his daily existence. "Can't leave her thinking something terrible has happened."

"Something terrible *has* happened," Raisa said, and heard the brittleness in her voice, felt the careful composure she'd maintained for sixty-seven years finally starting to fracture into pieces. "I drugged my granddaughter without her consent and somehow multiplied her into four people, and I have no idea how to explain this to my daughter without her thinking I've lost my mind or... or worse, understanding exactly what I did and never forgiving me for it."

The words hung in the warm kitchen air, stark and ugly and true. All four Kenzes had gone quiet, their attention finally captured by the distress in Raisa's voice. She saw the original one, the one with glasses, tilt her head in that characteristic way, confusion and concern crossing her face.

"Why would you need to explain it?" the original Kenz asked, and her voice had gone soft, uncertain. "We're fine, Grandma. We're all fine. We've been having fun, helping Mr. Fletcher and now we're at the farm and we're going to do chores and—"

"You're not supposed to be four of you," Raisa interrupted, hearing how her voice wanted to climb toward hysteria and forcibly pulling it back down. "There's supposed to be one Mackenzie. Just one. And I... I made a mistake, and now there are four, and I don't know how to fix it."

"Enough," Elizabeth said quietly, moving to Raisa's side and placing a warm hand on her shoulder. "Not now. Not with them listening and getting scared when they don't need to be scared yet. Samuel will take them to the barn. You'll call your daughter. I'll start working on understanding what happened so we can reverse it. One step at a time."

"But—"

"One step," Elizabeth repeated, and the firmness in her voice was the same gentle authority Samuel had used with the Kenzes, not harsh, not negotiable, just clear. "Samuel?"

He was already moving, already herding the four girls toward the door with the practiced efficiency of someone who'd managed children and animals in equal measure for decades. "Come on then. Barn chores won't wait for us to stand around talking. Chickens need feeding, eggs need collecting, and I expect you'll want to meet the goats."

"Goats!" Four voices in delighted unison, and just like that the Kenzes' attention pivoted completely, all worry forgotten in the face of new animals to meet. They scrambled for their shoes, jamming feet into sneakers without bothering to tie the laces properly, already peppering Samuel with questions about how many goats and what were their names and could they pet them and—

The door closed behind them and the kitchen fell into sudden quiet that felt almost shocking in its completeness. Raisa could hear the wood crackling in the stove, the soft hiss of the lamp on the table, her own breathing that had gone shallow and rapid without her noticing.

"Sit," Elizabeth said, pulling out a chair at the table. "Before you fall down."

Raisa sat because her knees agreed with Elizabeth's assessment. The chair's wooden seat was worn smooth, comfortable in the way that handmade things became after generations of use. She set her phone on the table in front of her and stared at it like it might offer some answer beyond the simple fact that she needed to call Claire and she had no idea what to say.

Elizabeth moved around the kitchen with the easy familiarity of her own space, setting a kettle on the stove, pulling mugs from their shelf, reaching for her herb jars with the precision of someone who could find what she needed in the dark. The sounds were soothing: water pouring, ceramic against wood, the soft scrape of a spoon measuring leaves.

"She'll want to know where Kenz is," Raisa said to the phone, to the table, to the warm kitchen air. "She'll want to come get her. And I can't... I can't let her see—"

"One true thing at a time," Elizabeth said, still moving through her preparations. "Kenz is safe. That's true. She's here at the farm with you. Also true. You're working on a situation and need until tomorrow. Still true, even if incomplete."

"Lying by omission."

"Protecting your daughter from panic about something you're actively working to resolve." Elizabeth set a mug in front of Raisa, steam rising from liquid the color of late summer honey. "Drink. It'll help you think clearly."

Raisa wrapped her hands around the mug's warmth and felt her phone vibrate against the table with another text, probably, or another call she was failing to answer. Her daughter's name appeared on the screen: *Calling...*

She picked up the phone before she could think better of it, before she could construct a perfect explanation that would satisfy without revealing. Sometimes you just had to step into the mess and trust you'd find your footing.

"Mom? Oh thank God, Mom, where have you been? I've been calling for hours and Martin Fletcher called me and said the weirdest thing about Kenz and—" Claire's voice came out in a rush, fear and relief and confusion all tangled together.

"I'm sorry," Raisa said, and meant it with every fiber of her being, even if Claire didn't know the full scope of what she was apologizing for. "My phone was on silent. There's been a... situation. With Kenz. But she's fine, she's safe, she's with me."

"What kind of situation? Martin said something about her volunteering with him, but he seemed really confused and kept asking if she had siblings, and I didn't understand what he was talking about and—"

"She's fine," Raisa repeated, forcing her voice into the calm, competent tone she'd relied on for sixty-seven years. "She got a little over-enthusiastic about helping in town and I had to go collect her. We're at the Miller farm now. You remember Elizabeth, my client? Kenz was interested in seeing the farm animals and it's been a long day, so we're staying here tonight."

The lie, or the incomplete truth, or whatever name made it easier to swallow, came out smoother than it should have. Raisa heard herself delivering it with the confidence of someone describing straightforward, reasonable events, even while her hands shook against the warm mug.

A pause on the other end. Then: "She's okay? Really okay? You'd tell me if something was wrong?"

Oh, the questions. If Raisa started telling the truth now, where would it end? *Well, actually, I drugged her with a magical potion because I couldn't handle her ADHD energy, and now there are four of her, but don't worry, we're working on a reversal...*

"She's really okay," Raisa said, and that much was true. The Kenzes were physically fine, happy even. "Just tired. And I think... I think I need tonight to process some things. Would it be all right if I brought her home tomorrow afternoon instead of this evening?"

Another pause, longer this time. Raisa could hear her daughter thinking, weighing, trying to decide if this was actually fine, or if she should push harder, demand more information, maybe even drive to the farm herself to see what was really happening.

"Okay," Claire said finally, slowly. "Okay, but Mom, you have to promise me, if something's wrong, if something's really wrong, you'll tell me? You won't just... manage it yourself?"

The irony was so sharp Raisa almost laughed. Wasn't that exactly what she was doing? Managing, controlling, trying to fix everything before anyone else had to know about her mistake?

"I promise," she said, adding another incomplete truth to the growing pile. "Get some rest. I'll call you tomorrow."

She ended the call before her daughter could ask more questions, before her voice could betray the exhaustion and fear and guilt all competing for space in her chest. Set the phone down on the table and stared at it like it might judge her for what she'd just done.

"That was the right call," Elizabeth said quietly, pulling out the chair across from Raisa and settling into it with her own mug of tea. "Giving yourself time to fix this before involving her. Sometimes protection means carrying burdens alone for a little while."

"Is that what I'm doing?" Raisa heard the bitterness in her voice. "Protecting her? Or protecting myself from having to admit what I did?"

Elizabeth was quiet for a moment, steam from her mug rising between them. Outside, through the kitchen window, Raisa could hear the faint sound of the Kenzes' voices from the barn, excited, overlapping, punctuated by Samuel's deeper tones offering instruction or correction.

"Maybe both," Elizabeth said finally. "Maybe that's allowed."

Raisa lifted the mug to her lips and drank, tasting chamomile and something else; lavender maybe, and a third flavor she couldn't quite identify but that settled warm and soothing in her chest. The tension in her shoulders eased fractionally, just enough for her to realize how much pain she'd been holding there.

"I need to start working," Elizabeth continued, pulling her grandmother's journal toward her and opening it to a marked page, "while Samuel has them occupied, but this will take time. Maybe all night. And I'm not..." She paused, choosing her words carefully. "I'm not certain I can reverse it by morning. This is unprecedented. I'll do everything I know how to do, but you need to be prepared for the possibility that tomorrow comes and there are still four Kenzes."

The words settled into Raisa's stomach like stones. Tomorrow. Her daughter expected her to bring Kenz home. The neighbors who'd seen four identical girls walking toward the square. Martin Fletcher who'd already raised questions. The farmer's market where the Kenzes had been enthusiastically "helping." Every hour that passed with the duplication unresolved was another hour the circle of witnesses expanded, another hour closer to a revelation Raisa couldn't control or contain.

"Then what?" she asked quietly. "If you can't reverse it? If they're... permanent? What do I tell my daughter? What do I tell anyone?"

Elizabeth reached across the table and covered Raisa's hand with her own warm one, stained with years of herb work, callused from farm labor, infinitely gentle. "Then we'll sort that out too. Together. One step at a time. But for now, you need to let me work, and you need to rest. The guest room is made up. Samuel will keep the girls busy until they wear themselves out, and then we'll settle them down somewhere they can sleep safely. You'll do no one any good collapsing from exhaustion."

Rest. As if Raisa could possibly sleep with four versions of her granddaughter running around the property and her daughter expecting answers tomorrow, and her entire carefully constructed life crumbling around her like poorly mixed mortar.

But she was so tired. Tired in a way that went beyond the physical, down into her bones and her heart and the places where she'd been holding herself together through sheer force of will for longer than she could remember.

"I'll stay here," she said, gesturing to the kitchen. "In case you need anything. In case—"

"In case you need to feel like you're doing something by hovering?" Elizabeth's voice held a gentle humor. "I work better alone, and you know it. Go. Rest. Trust that some problems can be solved without you managing every step."

The words landed harder than Elizabeth probably intended. Wasn't that the whole issue? Raisa's inability to let go, to trust, to accept that control was sometimes an illusion and often a cage? She'd tried to control Kenz's behavior and created four of her. What other disasters might she create if she kept insisting on managing everything herself?

She pushed back from the table and stood on legs that felt unsteady, leaving her mug half-finished and her phone face-down on the wooden surface. Through the window, she could see lamplight in the barn, could hear the faint sounds of evening chores and four enthusiastic voices offering help whether it was wanted or not.

Samuel would manage them. Elizabeth would work on the reversal. Raisa would... what? Rest? Let go? Trust in other people's competence when her own had failed so spectacularly?

She moved toward the door that led to the rest of the house, her feet finding the creaking floorboards that she'd heard countless times while waiting for Elizabeth to gather her things for medical appointments. The farmhouse wrapped around her with its scents of wood smoke and bread and generations of life lived simply, faithfully, in rhythm with seasons that turned whether you controlled them or not.

Behind her, she heard Elizabeth settling into her work. the sound of a page turning, and the soft scratch of pen on paper as she made notes. Purposeful sounds. Competent sounds. The sounds of someone who knew their craft and trusted their ability to find solutions through patient observation and careful experimentation.

Raisa paused in the doorway, one hand on the frame, looking back at Elizabeth's bent head in the lamplight. "Thank you," she said quietly. "For not—for just—"

"We'll talk about what you did later," Elizabeth said without looking up, her voice gentle but firm. "Right now, we solve the problem. The rest comes after."

Later. When there was time for reckoning, for moral judgment, for confronting exactly what Raisa had done and why. When the crisis had passed and nothing remained but the question of how to live with herself afterward.

But that was tomorrow's burden. Tonight, there was only this: a borrowed bedroom in a farmhouse that smelled like safety, four impossible granddaughters being worn out by evening chores, and a friend bent over her grandmother's journal in lamplight, searching for answers to questions that shouldn't need asking.

Raisa climbed the stairs toward the guest room and let the farm's quiet rhythms hold her, just for tonight, while Elizabeth worked and Samuel managed and the October darkness settled over everything like a blessing she hadn't earned but would accept anyway.

One step at a time. One breath. One moment of letting go.

It would have to be enough.

Chapter 8

As dawn light crept through the eastern windows, turning lamplight from necessity to comfort, Raisa sat at the long wooden table across from Elizabeth, surrounded by an archipelago of open books and journals, some bound in cracked leather that had absorbed decades of handling, others more recent paperbacks with creased spines and margin notes in Elizabeth's careful handwriting. Her own notebook lay before her, pages filling with observations she'd made about Kenz over the years, details she'd never thought to write down until now when they might matter, when they might be the difference between understanding and continued disaster.

She felt useful for the first time since watching that impossible green drop fall onto the cookie. The research gave her competence somewhere to anchor itself. She could contribute observations, cross-reference symptoms, help Elizabeth eliminate possibilities. This was work she understood: systematic investigation, careful documentation, the patient accumulation of data points that would eventually form a picture clear enough to act upon.

Elizabeth turned another page in her grandmother's journal, the paper so thin it was nearly translucent, covered in handwriting that shifted between English and what Raisa assumed was a German dialect the Amish in the area spoke. "Here," Elizabeth said, tapping a passage with one herb-stained finger. "Grandmother notes that the chamomile blend worked differently on restless children depending on whether their energy came from overstimulation or natural temperament. She had to adjust the proportions."

"How did she tell the difference?" Raisa asked, leaning forward to see the cramped notation even though she couldn't read half of it.

"Observation over time. Watching how they responded to quiet versus activity, to structure versus freedom." Elizabeth looked up, her brown eyes thoughtful in the lamplight. "The children whose restlessness came from too much happening around them would settle in calm environments. But the ones whose energy was just how they were made, those ones needed outlets, not suppression."

The words resonated uncomfortably. Raisa thought of all the times she'd tried to get Kenz to be still, to be quiet, to just slow down and focus. Had she been trying to suppress what was simply Kenz's natural state? The question sat heavy in her mind, but she pushed it aside to examine later. Right now, they needed to understand the mechanism, not her motivations.

"Kenz is the second type," she said. "Always has been. Even as a toddler, even when there was nothing stimulating happening, she'd be in motion. Not upset, just moving."

Elizabeth made a note, her pen scratching steadily across her own page. "And the medication she's on now, what does that do?"

"It helps her focus. Slows down the racing thoughts enough that she can finish tasks, follow conversations without getting derailed." Raisa paused, trying to articulate something she'd observed but never quite analyzed. "It doesn't make her less energetic, exactly. Just more... directed. Like it gives her brain enough traction to steer instead of just spinning."

"So it works with her nature, not against it." Elizabeth tapped her pen against the page, thinking. "That's important. The potion I gave you was designed the same way, to support the body's own efforts to find balance, not to impose calm from outside."

Raisa wondered, if the potion was designed to work with natural rhythms, why had it created such an unnatural result? Elizabeth's working theory was that something about Kenz's particular neurology had interacted unexpectedly with the formula. But what? ADHD itself couldn't be the answer. Elizabeth had used similar compounds successfully on adults with attention difficulties, restless energy, minds that wouldn't settle for sleep.

Outside the window, the sky was lightening properly now, the deep blue of predawn fading toward the pale gold of morning. Raisa could hear the household beginning to wake. There were footsteps above them, the creak of floorboards, low voices as the Miller children rose for their morning tasks. Soon Samuel would take the Kenzes - however many there were now, she'd lost track of whether four had become more during the night - out to help with animal care. The routine work would occupy them while Raisa and Elizabeth continued searching for answers.

The kitchen door opened and Samuel entered, already dressed for barn work, his presence somehow making the room feel more grounded just by virtue of his solid, unhurried calm. He moved to the stove and began preparing coffee with the ease of long practice, not speaking until the pot was filled and set to heat.

"The girls are waking," he said, pouring water into mugs for Raisa and Elizabeth without asking if they wanted any. "I'll take them for morning feeding and egg collection once they've eaten. Keep them occupied." He set the mugs down and studied the table covered in journals and notes. "You're making progress?"

"Some," Elizabeth said. "Still trying to understand why the reaction was so extreme."

Samuel nodded, unsurprised, and returned to the counter where he began assembling breakfast with the same methodical efficiency: bread, butter, jam, cheese, sliced apples. The simple domesticity of it filled Raisa's heart. This family had absorbed her disaster into their morning routine, making space for the impossible the way they made space for weather or sickness or any other challenge that required adaptation and steady work.

The children came down in a tumbling group, voices overlapping in the particular way of siblings who'd learned to communicate through layered conversation, followed shortly by the unmistakable sound of multiple Kenzes navigating the stairs with their characteristic combination of enthusiasm and imperfect coordination. Raisa's hands tightened around her coffee mug as she counted by ear. Still four, she thought, unless the sounds were deceiving her.

They burst into the kitchen in a wave of morning energy, all talking at once about dreams they'd had, and whether the chickens would remember them from yesterday, and did Samuel think the goats liked having help, and —

"Hands washed first," Samuel interrupted, not loudly but with enough firmness that nine children diverted toward the sink without argument. The Miller kids helped orchestrate the chaos, making sure everyone got a turn at the soap and water, directing the Kenzes toward open seats at the table once their hands met inspection.

Raisa watched the original Kenz, still distinguishable by her glasses, settle into a chair beside one of the Miller daughters, already chattering about how she'd dreamed she could fly but kept forgetting how to do it mid-flight which seemed really inconvenient. The other three Kenzes joined the conversation from their own seats, building on each other's thoughts in ways that made it impossible to tell where one ended and another began.

Four. Still four. The night had passed without new multiplication, which felt like a small victory even though Raisa knew it might just mean the process had paused rather than stopped.

Samuel distributed food with quiet efficiency, making sure each child had bread, and fruit, and cheese, pouring milk, and answering questions about the morning's work with the patient detail of someone who saw every task as a teaching opportunity. The Miller children ate steadily, listening to their father, while the Kenzes peppered him with enthusiasm about which tasks they could help with.

"You'll all work with me," Samuel said, settling the question before it could fragment into negotiation. "Chickens first, then goats, then we'll see what else needs doing. But you follow instructions exactly. No wandering off, no deciding to do something different because it seems interesting. Understood?"

"Yes, sir," the Kenzes chorused, then giggled at their synchronization.

Raisa met Elizabeth's eyes across the table and saw her own tentative hope reflected there. The structure was holding. The multiplication hadn't progressed. They had time to keep researching, to find the answer before—

Before what? Before her daughter showed up demanding explanations? Before the situation spiraled further beyond management? Before Raisa had to face the full weight of what she'd done?

She returned her attention to her coffee, to the journals, to the careful work of understanding. One step at a time. That was all she could manage.

The kitchen emptied as Samuel herded the collective children toward barn coats and morning chores, their voices fading as they crossed the yard. In the sudden quiet, Raisa felt the exhaustion of the sleepless night settle into her bones, but she pushed it aside. They were close to something, she could feel it. Some connection they hadn't quite made yet between Kenz's specific physiology and the potion's properties.

Elizabeth pulled another journal toward her, this one more recent, filled with her own experimental notes. "I've been thinking about the timing," she said. "When exactly did you first notice the duplication?"

Raisa had walked through this timeline multiple times, but she did it again, searching for details she might have missed. "The cookie was around twelve-thirty. I checked on her maybe twenty minutes later. Nothing unusual. Then I went back outside around one-twenty and there were two."

"So approximately fifty minutes after consumption." Elizabeth was making notes. "And the next multiplication from two to four happened while you were driving here to get me. How long was that?"

"Forty minutes? Maybe an hour?" The timeline felt slippery in her exhausted mind.

"And now we've gone all night without progression." Elizabeth tapped her pen thoughtfully. "Which suggests the process isn't continuous or inevitable. Something triggers each multiplication event."

The observation landed in Raisa's mind with the weight of significance, though she couldn't quite grasp why. Triggers. What had been different about those two moments when the duplication occurred versus the long stretches between?

They worked in companionable silence for another hour, the kitchen warming as the sun climbed higher, filling with light that made the lamplight unnecessary. Raisa's notebook pages accumulated her observations about Kenz; her energy patterns, her responses to different situations, the way sugar affected her differently than other kids, how she'd bounce off walls for hours after cake at birthday parties while other children settled down.

Sugar.

The thought arrived fully formed, so obvious she couldn't believe she hadn't seen it immediately. The cookie had been oatmeal raisin. Sweet. Loaded with sugar from the raisins and whatever sugar she'd mixed into the dough. And then Kenz had washed it down with lemonade more sugar. Raisa had watched her granddaughter consume what amounted to a sugar bomb minutes before the first multiplication.

"Elizabeth." Her voice came out hoarse from disuse. "The cookie had sugar in it. Quite a lot. Raisins, baked in, and then the lemonade—"

Elizabeth looked up sharply. "Sugar amplifies her? Makes her more energetic?"

"Dramatically." Raisa was already rifling through her notes, finding her earlier descriptions of Kenz's reactions. "Her mother learned years ago that sugar doesn't calm her down the way it does some ADHD kids. It winds her up, makes the ADHD symptoms even more intense. Racing thoughts, physical restlessness, everything just... more."

She watched Elizabeth's face change as the implications registered, saw the moment of understanding arrive with something that looked like horror.

"Oh no," Elizabeth said softly. "Oh, Raisa, no."

"What? What does that mean?"

Elizabeth was already pulling her grandmother's journal back toward her, flipping to passages she'd marked earlier. "The potion doesn't suppress or calm. It works with the body's natural rhythms, remember? It's designed to take whatever energy the person has and help them channel it productively. For anxious adults, that energy is nervous and scattered, so the potion helps them find focus and calm. But Kenz's energy—"

"Isn't nervous," Raisa finished, ice forming in her stomach. "It's expansive. That's what the doctor called it. Her ADHD manifests as expansive energy. Always more thoughts, more movement, more enthusiasm than she can process or channel alone."

"And you gave her a potion designed to work with and support that energy," Elizabeth said, her voice carrying the weight of terrible understanding. "Then amplified it with sugar. The magic did exactly what it was supposed to do. It took her expansive energy and gave it form. Physical, literal form."

The kitchen door opened before Raisa could respond, Samuel entering with his characteristic deliberate calm, but something in his expression made Raisa's stomach drop.

"We have eight now," he said quietly. "Counted twice to be certain. Eight."

The words hung in the air like smoke. Eight. The number felt impossible even though Raisa had watched four become reality, had driven them here, had listened to their overlapping voices through a late dinner and bedtime at the Miller's.

Eight Kenzes, all equally real, all equally her granddaughter, all existing because Raisa had tried to chemically suppress what she didn't understand.

"When?" Elizabeth was already on her feet. "When did you notice?"

"Just now, doing headcount before bringing them back in." Samuel moved to the window, looking out toward the barn. "Could be it happened earlier and I didn't notice. They scatter when I set them to tasks, hard to keep visual track of all of them at once."

Raisa joined him at the window, her legs unsteady, and saw what he saw: a cluster of strawberry blonde girls working in the kitchen garden plot, pulling weeds and talking in voices that carried across the intervening space. Eight of them. Eight versions of her granddaughter, moving and chattering and being Kenz in perfect multiplication.

"Breakfast," she heard herself say, the word coming from some analytical part of her brain that could still function while the rest spiraled. "They ate breakfast. Bread and jam. More sugar."

Samuel nodded slowly. "The jam was the sweet kind. The children like it better that way."

So that was the pattern. That was the trigger. Each time Kenz - each time any of them - consumed sugar, the amplification happened again, the expansive energy finding more physical form to fill because that's what the magic was designed to do: work with the body's natural state and expand it instead of fighting it.

Raisa had spent years knowing how sugar affected her granddaughter. She had reminded Claire countless times to limit sweets before events where Kenz needed to sit still or focus. Had watched firsthand as birthday cake transformed Kenz from merely energetic to absolutely manic. She'd known this. And she'd put that drop of potion on a sweet cookie and served it with sugary lemonade and never once connected those facts until the disaster had multiplied itself into eight identical children.

"We have to stop giving them anything sweet," she said, gripping the window frame for support. "Nothing with sugar until we can figure out reversal. If eight becomes sixteen—"

"I'll tell the children," Samuel said, already moving toward the door. "We'll switch to plain bread and cheese for meals. No fruit preserves, no honey, nothing sweet." He paused with his hand on the door. "And we'll keep them busy. Occupied. The less chaos we allow, the better."

He left them in the kitchen's yellow morning light, surrounded by journals that now made terrible sense, and Raisa felt something fundamental shift in her understanding of what she'd done. This wasn't a magical mishap or an unexpected chemical reaction. This was the potion working exactly as designed, taking Kenz's nature and supporting it, amplifying it, giving it room to expand in the only way magic knew how: literally.

She'd tried to suppress her granddaughter's ADHD with something designed to work with natural energy. She'd fed Kenz sugar, knowing it amplified her symptoms, then given her sugary peanut butter and jelly too.

And she'd given the cookie in secret, without consent, without understanding, acting from her own desperate need for control rather than any concern for Kenz's actual wellbeing.

The weight of it pressed down on Raisa's chest until breathing felt like lifting stones.

"We can fix this," Elizabeth said quietly from the table, though her voice carried less certainty than Raisa had ever heard in it. "Now that we understand what went wrong, we can work on a reversal that accounts for it. A formula that works with her ADHD instead of amplifying it. Something that gently consolidates rather than suppresses."

Raisa turned from the window to face her friend, saw her own exhaustion and guilt reflected in Elizabeth's face. "But the others," she said, voicing the question neither of them had wanted to examine too closely. "The seven others who weren't there yesterday morning. What happens to them when we reverse this? Are they... are we destroying seven aware beings? Or reintegrating divided consciousness?"

Elizabeth's hands moved to her grandmother's journal, touching it like a talisman or a prayer. "I don't know," she admitted. "That's the question I've been avoiding all night. My faith teaches that every soul is precious. But are they eight souls, or one soul divided into eight vessels? Does it matter morally which one is true?"

The kitchen clock ticked steadily, marking time they didn't have, counting down toward some moment when Raisa's daughter demand explanations or the neighbors would see too much or the multiplication would progress to numbers that couldn't be managed even with the Miller family's extraordinary capacity for organized chaos.

Raisa returned to the table and sank into her chair, staring at pages of notes that had seemed so productive an hour ago and now just documented the extent of her failure to understand. She'd thought herself so competent, so capable of managing any situation through careful planning and execution. But she'd never stopped to consider that maybe the situation didn't need managing. That maybe Kenz didn't need fixing. That her granddaughter's expansive energy was a feature, not a flaw, something to be channeled and celebrated rather than suppressed.

The potion had shown her that truth in the most literal way possible. It had taken her attempt at control and turned it into physical multiplication that couldn't be ignored or explained away.

"I need to tell her," Raisa said quietly. "Kenz. The real one, the original one. I need to tell her what I did. That I drugged her without permission because I couldn't handle who she is."

Elizabeth reached across the table and covered Raisa's hand with her own. "First we fix this. Then we reckon with it. One step at a time, remember?"

But Raisa shook her head, looking out the window at eight versions of her granddaughter working in the October garden, their voices carrying on the morning air in cheerful chaos. "She deserves to know. They all do. Before we try reversal, before we make any decisions about what happens next. They deserve the truth about how they came to exist."

The words settled between them, heavy with the weight of consequences Raisa had been trying to avoid but could no longer hide from. Outside, the Kenzes laughed at something one of them had said, the sound multiplied into a chorus that was both beautiful and heartbreaking.

Elizabeth squeezed Raisa's hand once, then released it and returned her attention to the journals. "Then we work fast," she said. "We find the solution quickly enough that when you tell them, you can also tell them how we're going to fix it. That's the kindness we can offer; truth paired with hope."

Raisa nodded, pulling her notebook back toward her, trying to focus on practical research when all she wanted was to put her head down on the worn wooden table and weep for her hubris, her rigidity, her determination to control what never needed controlling in the first place.

But weeping wouldn't multiply back into one child. Wouldn't restore what she'd fractured. Wouldn't undo the violation or return the consent she'd stolen.

Only understanding would do that. Understanding and work, and the terrible, necessary courage of admitting she'd been wrong about everything she'd thought she was doing right.

So she bent over the notebook and kept writing, kept documenting, kept searching for the answer that would let her face eight versions of her granddaughter and explain how her love had broken into this many pieces.

Chapter 9

Eight Kenzes. Eight versions of her granddaughter scattered across the Miller farm's various work zones, all talking at once, all moving with that characteristic unfocused enthusiasm, all completely unaware that seven of them shouldn't exist.

Samuel had the situation organized with the kind of calm efficiency that came from decades of managing five children and countless farm crises. He'd divided the eight girls into pairs, each supervised by one of his own children, and assigned them to different tasks spread across the property. The strategy was sound. Keep them separated enough that the chaos didn't compound exponentially, but give them real work that required focus and generated visible results.

Raisa stood in the barn's main aisle, holding a bucket of chicken feed she'd been tasked with distributing, and watched two Kenzes, neither wearing glasses, enthusiastically mucking out a goat pen under the patient supervision of the oldest Miller daughter. Their technique was terrible, all force and no finesse, but they were actually accomplishing something. The soiled straw was moving from inside the pen to the wheelbarrow, even if the path between the two locations involved considerable spillage.

"You're doing real good," the Miller girl said, her German accent softening the words. "Just remember to lift with your legs, not your back, yet. That's it."

One of the Kenzes paused mid-scoop, straw tumbling from her pitchfork as her attention snagged on something. "Did you know goats have rectangular pupils? I read about it somewhere, or maybe I saw it in a video, but anyway it helps them see predators coming from almost any direction, which is so cool because—"

"Keep working while you talk," the Miller girl interrupted gently. "Brain and body both at once."

And remarkably, it worked. The Kenz resumed her scooping, still chattering about goat biology, her hands continuing the motion even as her mind wandered. Raisa felt something; not quite hope, but recognition. The Miller girl wasn't trying to stop the talking, wasn't demanding quiet focus. She'd just redirected the energy, asked for coordination rather than suppression.

Samuel appeared at Raisa's elbow, manifesting with a farmer's stealth that came from decades of checking on things without startling livestock. "The ones in the garden need you," he said, nodding toward the kitchen plots visible through the barn's far door. "They're pulling weeds but can't tell which plants to keep. Elizabeth is too busy to supervise them."

Raisa set down the feed bucket and followed him across the yard, picking her way across gravel rutted by wagon wheels that probably needed raking but wouldn't get it today. Not with eight Kenzes requiring constant supervision, Elizabeth locked in her kitchen laboratory and the regular Miller children absorbed in management tasks that should have fallen to adults.

Two more Kenzes kneeled in the herb garden, their hands already dirt-stained, examining plants with the intense focus that characterized their hyperfocus moments. The original - she still wore her glasses, she noted with relief - looked up as she approached.

"Grandma! We're helping with the late-season harvest, but there are so many plants and I can't remember which ones Elizabeth said were the medicinal herbs versus the culinary ones, and this one smells amazing. What is it?" She thrust a handful of leaves toward Raisa's face.

"Lemon balm," Raisa identified automatically, then caught herself. She'd been about to explain that it was both culinary and medicinal, that Elizabeth dried it for calming tea, that it needed to be harvested before the first hard frost. But the Kenz - this Kenz, the original one who'd arrived at her house just yesterday morning, though it felt like decades ago - was already moving on, her attention caught by a bee investigating the last of the fall flowers.

"Oh wow, look at that bee! Is it collecting pollen this late in the year? Do bees know when frost is coming? I bet they have some kind of instinct about—"

"Hands," Raisa said, hearing Samuel's technique in her own voice. "Keep your hands moving. You can wonder about bees while you harvest."

To her surprise, it worked. Both Kenzes returned to their careful picking, fingers moving through the herb beds while their voices continued their overlapping commentary on bee behavior, frost timing, whether plants could feel the change of seasons, and had Raisa known that some perennials could live for decades?

Raisa kneeled beside them on the cold ground and began harvesting sage, showing them how to pinch the stems cleanly, how to leave enough growth for the plant to survive winter. Her back would complain about this later, but for now the physical work felt almost meditative. She couldn't solve the magical problem through competence or careful planning. She couldn't think her way to a reversal formula or control the outcome through sheer force of will. But she could do this: kneel in the dirt, clip herbs with steady hands, and keep two chaotic eleven-year-olds on task through gentle redirection.

It was something. It was more than she'd contributed since the moment she'd watched that impossible green drop fall onto the cookie.

The afternoon stretched and compressed in strange ways, time moving differently when measured in completed tasks rather than clock minutes. Raisa helped harvest herbs until the gathering baskets were full, then moved to the chicken yard where three Kenzes were collecting eggs under the supervision of two Miller children. The chickens seemed unbothered by the multiplication. They treated all the Kenzes with equal suspicion, squawking protests that were ignored with equal enthusiasm by all three girls.

"I got five eggs! No, wait, six! Oh, this one's still warm. That's so weird that eggs come out warm. I mean I know they do because they come from inside the chicken, but feeling it is different from knowing it, you know?"

Raisa knew. She was learning that knowing something intellectually and experiencing it physically were entirely different forms of understanding, and she'd been operating on the intellectual version for far too long.

Samuel appeared periodically to check progress, redistribute Kenzes when their energy flagged or spiked, and deliver the kind of brief, practical observations that served as both assessment and instruction. "The ones in the garden are doing good work. The goat pen is clean enough. Time to bring everyone in for a break and some water."

He gathered the scattered Kenzes with a series of calls, his voice carrying across the yard with practiced authority, and herded them toward the farmhouse where Elizabeth had been working all afternoon. Raisa followed the group inside, her hands dirt-stained and her back aching, and found the kitchen transformed into something between a laboratory and a library.

Elizabeth sat at the long wooden table, surrounded by open journals, measuring implements, small jars of dried herbs, and a mortar and pestle showing traces of green powder. Her grandmother's leather-bound book lay open beside a newer paperback on herbal chemistry, both covered in Elizabeth's careful annotations. She looked up as the chaos entered, her face showing the particular exhaustion that came from intense mental work, and managed a tired smile.

"Water and bread," she said, gesturing to the counter where Samuel had already set out a pitcher and a plate of plain sliced bread. There was no butter, no jam, nothing sweet that might trigger another multiplication event. "Sit quietly while you eat."

The eight Kenzes clambered onto benches around the table with less noise than Raisa would have predicted, their afternoon of physical work having burned off at least some of their boundless energy. They reached for bread with dirt-stained hands that Samuel redirected toward the washbasin first, creating a chaotic parade to the sink and back that somehow resolved into eight girls eating plain bread and drinking water while their voices created a wall of sound about chickens and goats and herbs and whether worms minded being dug up.

Raisa sank into a chair at the table's far end, accepting the mug of water Samuel handed her, and watched Elizabeth return to her work with the focused attention of someone who'd been deep in a problem for hours. The kitchen was warm from the wood stove, filled with the scent of drying herbs and bread, and also the smells of the farm that had worked its way into everyone's clothes; earth, and animals, and honest sweat.

***

Elizabeth's fingers ached from grinding herbs, from writing notes, from the careful measurement that herbalism demanded. The mortar held a fine powder that had taken twenty minutes to achieve. She needed consistency at almost a flour-like texture for the properties to extract properly in the tincture base. Her grandmother's journal lay open to a page discussing reversal techniques for over-amplified remedies, written in the mix of English and German that characterized the older woman's record-keeping.

When a formula works too well, the spidery handwriting read, *the reversal must account for why the excess occurred, not simply oppose the original intent.*

Elizabeth had read that passage eleven times now; each reading revealing new layers. The calming potion hadn't failed. It had succeeded too well, taking Kenz's expansive ADHD energy and amplifying it in the only way magic understood: literally. A reversal couldn't just suppress or cancel; it had to gently consolidate everything, bringing the expanded energy back to its original single expression without destroying what had been created, if that was even possible. If the seven other Kenzes were truly just overflow, just excess energy given temporary form, rather than...

She pushed the thought away and measured two parts valerian to one part chamomile, adding both to the mortar for a second grinding. The base calming herbs would help, but they needed something to encourage unity, to support the body's return to singular expression. Yarrow, maybe, for its traditional use in sealing wounds and bringing separated things together. But Yarrow worked on physical tissue, and this was metaphysical separation. Would the magic understand the symbolic parallel, or was she reaching?

Across the table, one of the Kenzes - the original, she though, with the glasses - asked Samuel a question about whether chickens dreamed, and Samuel answered with his characteristic brevity while the other seven Kenzes built on the question with their own tangents about bird brains and sleep cycles and whether dreams were memories or imagination.

Eight distinct voices. Eight separate streams of thought, each building on slightly different observations from the afternoon's work. The Kenz who'd mucked the goat pen was talking about goats. The one who'd watched the bee referenced pollination. They'd all started out as identical this morning, but six hours of separate experiences had begun creating divergence, subtle but unmistakable.

Elizabeth's hands stilled on the pestle. That was the question she kept avoiding, the one that made her faith clash uncomfortably with her practical knowledge. If each Kenz was having separate experiences, forming separate memories, developing separate understanding... did that make them separate people? Or were they still one consciousness experiencing eight simultaneous perspectives, ready to integrate back into unified memory when the reversal took effect?

Her beliefs taught that every soul was precious, that personhood was sacred, that life was a gift from God not to be taken lightly. But what constituted a person in this situation? How did divine creation intersect with magical multiplication? Were there eight souls now, where there had been one this morning? Or was it one soul spread across eight vessels, confused and fragmented but fundamentally singular?

And if it was the former, if those were truly eight distinct, conscious human beings sitting at her kitchen table eating bread and talking about chickens, what did it mean that she was preparing to collapse them back into one?

The pestle scraped against the mortar's interior, grinding herb powder finer, but Elizabeth's mind continued to grind against an ethical problem that had no clear answer in any journal or text.

Samuel appeared at her elbow, setting down a fresh mug of water she hadn't asked for but needed. His presence was steadying. It always had been, through twenty years of marriage and five children and countless farm crises that required faith and work in equal measure.

"You're troubled," he observed, not quite a question.

"The souls question," Elizabeth admitted quietly, glancing at the Kenzes to make sure they were too absorbed in their own conversation to listen. "I keep trying to work around it, focus on the practical chemistry, but I can't. If they're truly separate people now—"

"They're not," Samuel said with the certainty that came from his own observations. "Watch them.

Elizabeth realized Samuel had been watching the Kenzes all morning, the way he watched his fields for signs of pest damage or his livestock for subtle indicators of illness. You didn't manage a working farm for twenty-five years without developing the ability to notice patterns even before they fully formed.

The eight girls had spread across his property, working at various tasks, and he'd moved between the work zones checking progress and noting details. The way they moved, the way they thought, the structure of their chaos; he'd paid attention.

"See how they talk," he said to Elizabeth, keeping his voice low. "They all start each other's sentences. When one has a thought, the others pick it up mid-stream like they heard the beginning even when they were across the yard."

Elizabeth looked up from her grinding, attention shifting to the Kenzes with the focused observation he was encouraging. At the table's far end, the conversation about chickens had somehow morphed into speculation about whether plants could communicate, and the eight voices were weaving together in ways that suggested a shared rather than a separate consciousness.

"—because I read somewhere that trees share nutrients through their roots, and if trees can do that then maybe—"

"—other plants can too, like maybe the herbs in the garden are all connected underground and that's why—"

"—they grow better in groups than alone, because they're helping each other or sharing information about—"

"—when to flower or when frost is coming or—"

One thought passed between eight mouths, each picking up the thread seamlessly, building on it, returning it to the collective pool for the next speaker to catch. It wasn't a conversation in the usual sense. It wasn't eight individuals discussing a topic. It was one mind thinking out loud through eight voices, the way someone might pace while working through a problem, moving physically to support the mental process.

"They're not forming separate memories," Samuel continued, watching Elizabeth's face as understanding dawned. "They're forming one shared memory of eight simultaneous experiences. Come evening, when you ask them about their afternoon, they'll all answer because they all remember all of it. The one who mucked goats knows about collecting eggs. The one in the herb garden knows about the chickens."

He'd tested this theory an hour ago, asking the Kenz who'd been in the barn about the bee the gardening Kenz had seen, and she'd answered with the same detail and enthusiasm as if she'd observed it personally. Because she had, in a sense. They all had. One consciousness experiencing reality through eight sets of eyes, eight positions in space, eight slightly different vantage points on the same continuous experience.

Elizabeth's hands had gone still on her work. "So, the reversal won't be destroying seven people," she said slowly, relief and remaining uncertainty mixing in her voice. "It'll be reintegrating one person who's been temporarily... spread out."

"That's my observation," Samuel agreed. "But I'm not a scholar of souls or magic. I just know farming and children, and I know when something is one thing scattered versus many separate things gathered."

The distinction mattered, he understood, even if he couldn't articulate why in theological terms the way Elizabeth could. His faith was simpler, more practical. God made the world according to certain principles, and those principles held even when magic got involved. A person was a person, indivisible in the ways that mattered, even if temporary circumstances created the appearance of multiplication.

The work ahead was reintegration, not destruction. Bringing scattered pieces back to wholeness. That sat easier with his conscience than the alternative.

Raisa listened to Samuel's explanation and felt something lift, though she couldn't quite name it as relief. The ethical question had been hovering at the edges of her awareness all morning, surfacing whenever she looked at eight identical granddaughters and tried to imagine choosing which one counted as real. If Samuel was right, and his observations about the shared consciousness aligned with things she'd noticed but not synthesized, then the reversal wasn't an impossible choice. It was a repair.

"So, when Elizabeth administers the reversal," she said slowly, working through the implications, "she'll be helping Kenz come back together. Not erasing seven versions, but consolidating one temporarily expanded person?"

"That's the theory," Elizabeth said, returning to her grinding with renewed purpose. "Though I'm working from observation and hope more than established precedent. My grandmother's journal has notes on reversal techniques, but nothing about human multiplication because apparently I'm the first in three generations to encounter this particular disaster."

The dry humor in her voice was gentle, without edge, and Raisa felt simultaneously grateful for Elizabeth's refrain from judgment and ashamed that she deserved more condemnation than she was receiving. She'd created this disaster.

And now Elizabeth was spending her day grinding herbs and consulting arcane journals, Samuel was reorganizing his entire farm operation around supervising eight chaotic children, the Miller kids had sacrificed their normal routine to help manage a crisis they bore no responsibility for, and Raisa sat here with aching hands and a guilty conscience, contributing what she could, but knowing it would never be enough to balance what she'd taken.

"I need to tell her," Raisa said quietly, watching the original Kenz, at least, the one she believed was original based solely on the glasses, laugh at something one of the Miller children had said. "Before we do the reversal. She deserves to know what I did. Why this happened."

Elizabeth looked up, her brown eyes serious. "After we fix it," she said firmly. "Give yourself something to offer alongside the confession. 'I made a terrible mistake and here's how we fixed it' is different from 'I made a terrible mistake and we're still drowning in consequences.'"

"Is that ethics or kindness?" Raisa heard the bitterness in her own voice.

"Both," Elizabeth said simply. "Same as most things worth doing."

The kitchen had grown quieter, Raisa realized. The Kenzes' constant chatter had diminished to sleepy murmurs, their long morning of physical work finally catching up with them. Several had their heads pillowed on their arms at the table, still talking but with the loose, unfocused quality of children fighting sleep they didn't want to admit they needed. The Miller children were clearing bread plates and water cups with the efficient teamwork of a family that had worked together for years.

Samuel caught Elizabeth's eye and jerked his head toward the door in silent communication. Elizabeth looked up from her notes and gave a small, sharp shake of her head.

He crossed to her side of the table, lowering his voice. "They need rest. The ones in the barn this morning were already dragging before lunch."

"They need the reversal more," Elizabeth said, just as quietly. "Raisa has to have Kenz home by this evening. One whole Kenz, not eight tired ones." She glanced at her formula notes, then at the small vial sitting at the table's edge. "And I'm ready. The formula is done."

The words dropped into the kitchen's relative quiet with the weight of everything that had led to them. Raisa straightened in her chair.

Samuel looked at the vial, then at his wife, then at the row of drowsy Kenzes, and made the calculation that was second nature to a farmer: what needed to happen, in what order, before the light ran out. "Then we do it now," he said. "While they're calm. Tired and calm is better than rested and scattered."

"That's actually correct," Elizabeth said, and something in her voice caught, the sound of a theory confirming itself. "Samuel, that's exactly right." She reached for her journal and opened it to the page dense with the morning's annotations. "My grandmother's notes on consolidation; she wrote that energy returns to center most readily when it's already quieted. I kept thinking we needed them alert, coordinated. But calm is closer to singular than active is."

She was already on her feet, moving to the dry goods shelf where she kept her prepared materials. "We need them all in one place. Seated, unhurried. We don't tell them to pay attention or focus. We just give them each their portion and let them be tired together."

Samuel nodded once and turned to his children, speaking in German, quick and quiet. The older two straightened and began the careful work of consolidating the eight Kenzes from their various positions of sprawl, a hand on a shoulder here, and a gentle redirection there, gathering them toward each other at the long table without announcement or urgency.

Raisa stood but didn't move to help. She understood, watching Samuel's children work, that her role right now was to stay out of the way and not introduce her anxiety into a room that needed to stay calm.

"Before we do this," she said, when the last Kenz had been settled, eight pairs of half-drowsy eyes arranged in a loose arc around the table, "I need to tell them something."

Elizabeth paused, the vial in her hand. She looked at Raisa and waited.

Raisa pulled out the chair at the head of the table and sat down so she was level with them rather than standing over them. Eight faces looked on, each wearing a version of the same expression: tired, curious, a little uncertain about why everyone was being so deliberate.

"I owe you an explanation," she said, directing it to all of them, but finding the one with glasses and holding her gaze there. "What happened - the reason there are eight of you instead of one - is my fault. I put something in your cookie yesterday without asking you, without telling you. A drop from a vial Elizabeth gave me. I thought it would help you be calmer while we worked in the garden." She made herself continue through the flinch she felt at her own words. "I thought I was helping. But I was trying to change who you are without your permission, and that was wrong. The multiplication happened because of what I did."

The kitchen was very quiet. One of the Kenzes, not the one with glasses, was the first to speak. "The oatmeal raisin cookie? With the lemonade?"

"Yes."

A pause while eight minds processed this through the shared current Samuel had identified. Then the original said quietly: "I wondered why you were watching me eat it."

Raisa had no answer for that.

"We're not mad," said another, in the matter-of-fact tone of someone reporting a fact rather than offering comfort. "I mean, it's been kind of a lot. But also we got to see inside goat-thought, essentially, and that's something."

A murmur of agreement ran around the table, the Kenzes' characteristic ability to find the interesting angle on any situation operating even through exhaustion and revelation.

"You should still be mad," Raisa said. "That's allowed."

The one with glasses looked at her steadily. "Can we be mad later? After we're one person again?"

"Yes," Raisa said. "After."

Elizabeth stepped forward then, efficient and gentle, distributing the small measured portions into eight cups of plain water carrying a green-tinted fraction of the whole while Samuel and his children positioned themselves quietly around the room, unhurried and present. No one was restrained. No one was told to focus. The Kenzes held their cups the way tired children hold things, loosely, without drama.

"All together," Elizabeth said. "When you're ready. There's no rush."

They drank together, not quite simultaneously, one a half-second behind the others, one who drained hers and then looked at the empty cup with academic interest. Finally, the cups came down and the kitchen was quiet, and everyone waited.

Raisa watched her granddaughter's face. All eight of them. The drowsiness that had been pulling at them all through the basic lunch meal seemed to deepen, but gently, the way sleep comes when you finally stop fighting it. No distress. No alarm. Just eight versions of one child settling into something more still than they'd been all day, the constant low hum of their energy quieting to a frequency Raisa could almost feel rather than hear.

She didn't realize she was holding her breath until Elizabeth's hand came to rest briefly on her shoulder.

Whatever was going to happen would happen, or it wouldn't. She had done the last thing available to her: told the truth, and stepped back, and let Elizabeth's careful work take over.

Outside the kitchen window, the October afternoon was burning down toward a long, slanted evening light that meant she had only a few hours left. It was enough time, if this worked, to drive home with one Kenz, to make a phone call to her daughter, to begin the longer and harder work of repair.

She would figure out what to say on the way.

CHAPTER 10

One minute. Two. The kitchen clock's ticking seemed unnaturally loud.

One of the Kenzes made a small sound. It wasn't distressed, just surprised, and Raisa's attention snapped to her. The girl's outline had gone slightly soft, like looking at her through water or old glass. Not disappearing, not fading, just... blurring at the edges in ways that made Raisa's eyes hurt trying to focus.

"It's working," Samuel said quietly, and Raisa realized all eight girls were showing the same effect now, their forms losing the sharp definition of separate bodies.

The blurring increased. Where there had been clear space between the eight bodies, now there seemed to be something connecting them, threads of similarity drawing together.

The change, when it came, was visible. Not dramatic. No light, no sound, nothing that would have announced itself to anyone not already watching, but Raisa was watching, had been watching since eight cups were set down and eight pairs of eyes went soft with something between tiredness and something she had no name for. And she saw the moment it started.

The edges of them went uncertain.

Not blurry; more like her eye's instinct to track a single person kept losing its footing, sliding from one Kenz to the next as though they were all equally valid candidates for the same point in space. She blinked. Tried to count. Beside her she felt Samuel go still.

Seven. Six. The number kept slipping.

They weren't moving physically. They sat in their chairs, hands loose, none of them speaking now, but something about them was converging, some quality that had been distributed across eight bodies was concentrating back toward a center. The room felt smaller. Elizabeth stood motionless at the edge of it, hands clasped, watching.

Then the one with glasses made a small sound and pressed both palms flat on the table.

And the compression reversed.

Eight chairs. Eight girls. The room snapped back to itself, and all of them were looking at their hands or the table or at each other with expressions that ranged from dazed to frightened, and Raisa was already crossing to the original before she'd decided to move.

"Something happened," the girl said. Her voice was careful, like she was testing whether words still worked.

"Yes." Raisa put her hands on her granddaughter's shoulders. "It didn't finish. But you're not in danger."

Elizabeth reached the table in three strides and crouched to the original's eye level, her herbalist's assessment moving quickly across the girl's face, her pupils, the set of her jaw. "Did it hurt?"

"No. It felt like—" Kenz stopped and tried again, "like I almost remembered something and then forgot it before I could."

Elizabeth stood. Raisa recognized the expression on her face, the one that meant a theory was reorganizing itself at speed. She crossed back to her notes without a word, and Raisa heard pages turning.

"The water," Elizabeth said.

Raisa turned. "What?"

"The water." Elizabeth was already writing, her hand moving fast. "I put the formula in water because I didn't want to risk another multiplication event. But the potion was never meant to be delivered that way. It works with the body's natural state. I wrote that myself in chapter four of my grandmother's notes, I've read it a dozen times in the last two days." She looked up, and her expression held the particular showed the frustration of someone who'd been standing in front of an answer for hours. "Sugar doesn't just amplify Kenz's energy. It's the medium the potion knows how to work through. That's why it multiplied when she ate the cookie and the lemonade both. The formula was doing exactly what it was designed to do — following the body's rhythms. And those rhythms needed sugar to carry it."

The silence in the kitchen had a quality of held breath.

"So the reversal—" Raisa started.

"Needs the same carrier." Elizabeth closed the journal. "It won't scramble the memories or cause another multiplication. The formula is a reversal compound, not the original potion. But it needs to travel through the same pathway that the original did. Something sweet. A small amount, enough to carry it, not enough to trigger anything on its own." She was already moving toward the pantry. "Hopefully, we have some honey."

"Second shelf," Samuel said.

It took Elizabeth twelve minutes to prepare the adjusted doses. Raisa watched her work with the attention of someone who understood she was seeing the thing that would either fix this or confirm it was unfixable. The honey went in last, a small measured spoonful stirred into each portion until the liquid ran a faint amber rather than the near-clear it had been before. Not sweet enough to be a treat. Sweet enough to matter.

The Kenzes, still unsettled from whatever they'd almost experienced, accepted the fresh cups with less chatter than they'd shown all day. The original held hers in both hands and looked at Raisa over the rim.

"Is this going to work?" she asked.

"We think so," Raisa said, which was the truest, most honest answer available.

"Okay." She drank.

The others followed, and Raisa stood back and watched and did not look away.

This time the change was slower. Not a compression, more like a tide going out, gradual and inevitable, the edges of each duplicate becoming less insistent about their own boundaries. Raisa kept her eyes on the one with glasses, who sat with her hands in her lap and her eyes open, and watched her granddaughter's face move through a series of expressions she couldn't name. Not fear, not pain, but something more like the look of someone integrating a long and complicated dream into their waking understanding of the world.

The count reduced. Four. Three. Raisa didn't blink.

When there was one, there was not a collapse, not a snap, just a gradual settling into a singularity.

Kenz sat at the long table in the Miller kitchen with her glasses slightly askew and her hair a disaster from a full day of farm work, and she was alone, and she was entirely herself, and she looked up at Raisa with the expression of someone who had just returned from somewhere very far away.

"Oh," she said softly. "I remember all of it."

Raisa crossed to her and sat down beside her, but she didn't trust herself to speak.

"I was in the barn," Kenz said, half to herself, working through it. "And in the garden. And collecting eggs. And I remember all of it the same, like it all happened to me, because it did." She paused. "That's a lot of morning."

From somewhere behind Raisa, she heard one of the Miller children exhale. Samuel said something quiet in German and Elizabeth answered him. The others in the kitchen began to move again. The cups were collected, and the benches pushed back. There were all the ordinary sounds of people resuming life in their world after holding still for something extraordinary.

Raisa was looking at her granddaughter.

One granddaughter. Eleven years old. Glasses, dirt on her collar, a fresh scrape on her left elbow that Raisa hadn't noticed until now. Still Kenz. Still entirely, exhaustingly herself, but sitting with a quality of quiet that wasn't suppression or sedation. Just someone who had experienced a great deal and was taking a moment to absorb it.

"We need to talk," Raisa said. "About how this happened. What I did."

Kenz stared at her. "I know you put something in the cookie."

"Yes."

"You said that before." She didn't sound angry. She sounded like someone who had been thinking about a thing from many angles simultaneously, which was exactly what had happened. "I want to hear you say it, though. All of it."

"You will," Raisa said. "In the car. On the way home." She paused. "I'm taking you home today. To your mother. And I'm going to tell her what happened too."

Something moved through Kenz's expression. Surprise, maybe, or the recalibration of an expectation. Then a small, careful nod.

"Okay," she said. "Yeah. Okay."

Outside the kitchen window, the October afternoon was burning down toward early evening, long gold light stretching across the Miller fields. Enough time. Barely, but enough.

Raisa stood, and reached out her hand, and her granddaughter took it.

Chapter 11

Elizabeth's hands squeezed her shoulders gently. "How do you feel?"

Kenz seemed to weigh the question. "Full," she said finally. "Like I'm all of me now instead of being spread out. But also like I remember being spread out, and that's really weird, but also kind of amazing?"

"I remember everything," Kenz said quietly as she looked back at her grandmother. "All eight of everything."

Raisa felt the words land like a stone. "I know," she heard herself say, her voice rough with mounting guilt. "Kenz, I'm so sorry—"The apology stuck in her throat, too large and too inadequate at once.

Elizabeth stepped smoothly into the silence. "Let's give you some space to rest before you have to go," she said to Kenz, her hands still steady on the girl's shoulders. "This was a lot for your mind and body. Samuel will get you settled somewhere quiet."

Samuel moved forward with his characteristic calm and guided Kenz toward the door, one hand hovering near her elbow in case the reintegration had left her physically unsteady. The Miller children followed, their voices already asking careful questions about what it had felt like, whether she could really remember eight mornings at once, and if the memories would fade or stay.

The kitchen emptied until only Raisa and Elizabeth remained in the afternoon light, surrounded by empty glasses and the tools of successful reversal. Elizabeth began gathering her notebooks. She moved efficiently through the familiar task, but Raisa could see the exhaustion in the set of her shoulders, and the weight of what she'd accomplished.

"Thank you," Raisa said, inadequate words for an impossible debt. "Elizabeth, I can never--"

"You can," Elizabeth interrupted gently, pausing in her cleanup to meet Raisa's eyes. "You can by learning from this. By being different with her going forward. By remembering that love without acceptance isn't actually love at all."

She lifted the original vial, the one that had started everything, still over half-full of green liquid that glowed faintly in the sunlight from the window. "This needs to be disposed of properly. Returned to the earth with acknowledgment of what it can do, what it did." Her mouth tightened slightly. "I should have asked more questions before giving it to you. I should have required more safeguards. This was my mistake too."

"You gave it to me with explicit instructions about consent," Raisa said. "I'm the one who ignored them."

"We both have things to answer for." Elizabeth wrapped the vial carefully in cloth and set it aside. "But right now, you have a conversation to have with your granddaughter. And Raisa, she'll understand. Maybe more than you think."

The goodbyes happened in stages as the afternoon stretched toward evening. The Miller children hugged Kenz with genuine affection, trading addresses so they could write letters. They weren't permitted to have phones, but correspondence was encouraged. Samuel shook Raisa's hand with his characteristic firm grip and simple words: "You're welcome back, yet. Anytime."

Elizabeth walked them to the van, her arm around Kenz's shoulders in the easy affection that came naturally to her. "Remember what you learned," she said to the girl," about yourself, about your energy, about how to hold it. That's knowledge worth keeping."

Kenz nodded seriously, then surprised Elizabeth with a fierce hug that the older woman returned without hesitation. When they separated, Kenz's eyes were bright with tears she was trying not to shed.

Raisa found her own throat tight as she embraced Elizabeth. "I still don't know how to thank you."

"By doing better," Elizabeth said simply. "That's all any of us can do. Recognize our mistakes and choose differently next time."

The drive began in silence. Raisa navigated the familiar roads while Kenz sat in the passenger seat, not bouncing, not chattering, just looking out the window at October fields going dormant for winter. The quality of her stillness was different from suppression, Raisa noticed. This was attention, focus, the kind that came from integration rather than exhaustion.

Finally, when they'd left the farm's gravel roads behind for the paved county highway, Raisa spoke.

"I need to apologize to you. Really apologize, not just say I'm sorry." She kept her eyes on the road but felt Kenz's attention shift toward her. "What I did was wrong. I drugged you without your knowledge or consent because I couldn't handle your energy, because I wanted you to be easier to manage, because I put my own comfort ahead of your autonomy."

The words felt inadequate even as she spoke them, but she forced herself to continue. "I told myself I was helping you. That if you were calmer, our time together would be more pleasant for both of us. But I was really just trying to control you. To make you fit into my rigid expectations instead of accepting who you actually are."

Kenz was quiet for a long moment. Then: "I know why you did it. Not that I'm saying it's okay, but I understand now. I experienced myself from outside and it's—" She paused, searching for words. "I'm a lot. I know I'm a lot. I remember being so enthusiastic about helping in your garden and also being one of the versions of me who had to replant everything I destroyed. I felt how much work I created while trying to help."

"That doesn't excuse what I did," Raisa said firmly.

"No," Kenz agreed. "It doesn't. But I also understand that I'm really hard for people to handle sometimes, and you didn't have the tools to manage that, so you tried to find one. You just chose the wrong tool."

The wisdom in her granddaughter's voice made Raisa's eyes sting. Eleven years old and speaking like someone who'd lived multiple lifetimes simultaneously — which, in a way, she had.

"I'm not going to try to manage you anymore," Raisa heard herself promise. "I'm going to try to accept you and support you without trying to fix you. Give you stable ground to be yourself from instead of trying to calm you down to what I can handle."

"I think I can try to be more careful too," Kenz offered quietly. "Not like, stop being myself. But I understand now what my energy does, how it affects people and spaces. That's worth knowing even if it's uncomfortable to know."

They drove in silence for another mile, the countryside giving way to suburban development. Raisa's hands were steady on the wheel, but her thoughts were already ahead of them, at Claire's door, on Claire's face when she opened it.

"I need to call your mother," Raisa said. "Let her know we're coming."

Kenz turned from the window. Something in her expression told Raisa she'd been waiting for this part. "What are you going to tell her?"

"The truth." Raisa heard herself say it without hesitation, which surprised her. "All of it."

Kenz was quiet for a moment. "She's going to be really upset."

"Yes."

"At you or at me?"

"At me," Raisa said. "This is not your fault. None of what happened was your fault, and I need you to hold onto that while your mother and I talk."

She pulled into a gas station parking lot, put the van in park, and picked up her phone. Kenz watched but didn't speak, which was its own kind of consideration.

Claire answered before the first ring finished. "Where are you? I've been calling since this morning."

"We're about twenty minutes away." Raisa kept her voice level. "I'm bringing Kenz home."

"Is she all right? What happened? You said one day, Mom, you said you'd have her back by—"

"She's sitting right here. She's physically fine." Raisa chose the word deliberately. "I need to talk to you when we get there. In person."

"You're scaring me."

"I know. I'm sorry." She paused. "I did something I shouldn't have. I need to tell you what it was."

The silence on the other end stretched in a way that told Raisa her daughter was recalibrating, trying to decide what category of disaster this was. "How bad?"

"Bad enough that I'm not asking you to wait until tomorrow to hear it."

Claire's exhale was audible. "Twenty minutes."

"Twenty minutes," Raisa confirmed, and ended the call.

Kenz was looking at her hands in her lap. "She sounded scared."

"She's been scared since yesterday," Raisa said. "That's my fault too."

She pulled back onto the road and didn't say anything else. The truth would have to speak for itself when they got there.

Chapter 12

The porch light was on at Claire's house, and the door opened before they reached the steps.

Claire looked at Kenz the way mothers look at children returned from somewhere frightening from top to bottom and back again, cataloguing.

Whatever she saw satisfied the most urgent question because her shoulders dropped fractionally. Then she looked at Raisa, and her expression was considerably less relieved.

"Come in," she said.

The kitchen table. Raisa had known it would be the kitchen table. Claire's instinct under stress was the same as hers, put people in chairs, give hands something to hold. Three mugs appeared, though Raisa noticed Claire didn't ask what anyone wanted. Her movements were controlled in a way that meant she was managing something underneath them.

"Kenz," Claire said, still looking at Raisa, "can you go upstairs for a little while?"

"I'd actually like her to stay," Raisa said. "She was part of this. She deserves to hear me tell it."

Claire's jaw tightened slightly. She looked at her daughter, who gave a small, serious nod, and then she sat down. "All right. Tell it."

So, Raisa told it.

She got as far as the cookie, the drop from the vial, the deliberate choice, the fact that she had not told Kenz what she was doing, before Claire's hand came flat down on the table.

"Stop." Her voice was very quiet. "You put something in her food?"

"Yes."

"Without telling her?"

"Yes."

Claire stared at her. The silence had an edge to it that Raisa recognized from Claire's adolescence, from the moments when her daughter's anger ran too deep for immediate words. "You drugged my child?"

"Yes." Raisa did not soften it or redirect it. "That's what I did."

Claire stood up, and for a moment she simply stood there, hands on the back of her chair, looking at nothing. Then she said, "Keep going. I want to hear all of it."

Raisa kept going. She described coming back to the garden to find two Kenzes working side by side.

"No," Claire said flatly. "Stop. Two."

"Two."

"You're telling me there were two of her?"

"Yes."

"Mom." Claire's voice had taken on the careful tone of someone deciding whether to call for help. "That isn't... people don't do that. Children don't... that's not possible, not something that happens."

"I know. And then there were four."

Claire sat back down. "There were not four!"

"There were. And then when we reached the Miller farm—"

"You're saying you took four children who all looked like my daughter to an Amish farm and didn't call me."

"I called you that evening—"

"You told me she was fine and staying overnight." Claire pressed both hands flat on the table. "How many?"

Raisa met her daughter's eyes. "Eight."

The kitchen was very quiet.

"I need you," Claire said slowly, "to explain to me what you think happened. Because what you're describing is not possible, and I'm trying to figure out if you're having some kind of episode, or if—" She looked at Kenz. "Tell me what you remember."

Claire looked at her daughter. Kenz, to her credit, nodded steadily. "I remember all of it," she said. "All eight of me. I was in the barn, and the herb garden, and the chicken yard and, well, it was a lot, but it all happened."

Claire picked up her mug and put it down without drinking from it. "You're telling me that my mother gave you a magic potion—"

"A herbal compound," Raisa said, and immediately recognized the instinct for what it was, the same one that had made her call it helping instead of drugging. "I'm sorry. That's not a meaningful distinction."

"—and it multiplied you into eight people?" Claire looked at Kenz. "And you remember being all of them?"

"It was more like being one person in eight places at once," Kenz said. "Like — " She considered. "Like if you could be in the kitchen and the living room and upstairs at the same time, and you could see everything happening in all of them, except it was also all just you."

Claire sat with that for a moment. "And Elizabeth Miller reversed it?"

"Yes," Raisa said. "After two days and one failed attempt. The formula worked on the second try."

"Two days." Something shifted in Claire's voice. "I called you eleven times today, Mom. When you bothered to answer at all, you kept telling me she was fine."

"She was physically safe. I didn't lie about that."

"You let me spend a day and a half—" Claire stopped. Started again, more carefully. "I thought she'd broken something. I thought maybe she'd wandered off, and you were embarrassed to tell me. I thought you'd had a medical event and were covering it up." Her voice had gone very even, which Raisa knew was worse than raised. "I did not think my mother had secretly dosed my daughter with a magic potion and multiplied her into eight people and then lied to me while I sat here alone trying to figure out what was wrong."

Raisa absorbed this without deflecting. It was exactly what had happened, and there was nothing to add to it.

"I'm sorry," she said. "For the choice I made with the potion, and for not telling you the truth when you called. Both of those were wrong. I was trying to fix the problem before you had to know about it, and I understand now that wasn't my decision to make."

"No," Claire said. "It wasn't."

Kenz reached across the table and put her hand over her mother's. Claire turned her hand over and held on without looking away from Raisa.

"I need you to understand something," Claire said finally. "Whatever is going on with you and Kenz, whatever you're struggling with when she visits, whatever it is that made you desperate enough to do this, I needed to know about that. I've been trying to figure out why the visits have gotten harder, why Kenz comes home quieter than she left. I thought it was something I was doing wrong."

Raisa felt that land exactly as hard as it deserved to. "It wasn't. It was never anything you did wrong."

"Then why didn't you talk to me?"

There was no clear answer to that. Only the same answer she'd been sitting with for two days: the one about control and fear and the deep instinct to manage everything alone rather than admit she was struggling. She said as much, plainly, without dressing it up.

Claire listened. When Raisa finished, she was quiet for long enough that the heat had gone out of the untouched tea.

"I don't know what to do with all of this right now," Claire said at last. "I'm not... I can't tell you it's fine tonight. It isn't."

"I know," Raisa said. "I'm not asking for that."

"I need some time."

"That's fair."

Claire looked at her daughter again giving her a long, assessing look. Something in her softened, just slightly. "You really remember all eight... bodies, all eight days you had?"

Kenz almost smiled. "I really do. I'll tell you about the goats sometime. The goats were actually really interesting."

Something moved across Claire's face that wasn't quite a smile, but was nearly one. She didn't release Kenz's hand.

Raisa wrapped both palms around her cold mug and let the situation be what it was: not resolved, not repaired, but honest. The truth was on the table, and it belonged to all three of them now, which was where it should have been from the beginning.

The kitchen went quiet in a way that felt, for the first time in two days, like rest rather than held breath.

Then Kenz said, "I know this is probably not the right moment, but I haven't eaten anything except plain bread and water since this morning and I'm actually really hungry. Like, really, really hungry. Is there any pasta? Or soup? Or honestly anything that isn't plain bread?"

Claire looked at her daughter for a moment, and then something in her face gave way — not quite a laugh, not quite a sob, but something that lived in the narrow space between them. She pushed back from the table and went to the refrigerator.

"There's leftover chicken," she said, her voice slightly unsteady. "And I can make rice."

"That sounds amazing," Kenz said, with a feeling that suggested she genuinely meant it. "I helped collect eggs today. All eight of me did, actually. I'll tell you about it while you cook."

Raisa wrapped both hands around her cold mug and stayed where she was, watching her daughter move through the familiar motions of feeding her child, and let the ordinary sounds of the kitchen settle around her like something she hadn't known she was missing.

Afterward

In the summer of 2025, I woke up early one morning from a strange dream with all too real elements.

A family member who drives for the Amish from time to time, who has cultivated friendships with several of them, has had my neurodiverse daughter – Kenz – help her at her house doing weeding and other such tasks as Raisa has Kenz 'help' her in this story. As with the Kenz of the story, sometimes the wrong thing gets pulled, and sometimes Kenz's ADHD is hard for my family member to manage.

The dream was about her driving one of her Amish ladies and having the woman suggest a little help for her to manage Kenz. In my dream, Kenz doubled right away, as she ate the cookie. My family member didn't let her/them go back outside to the flower beds. She went to get her Amish friend and, when they got back, they found the two Kenz's gone.

The two women found four Kenz's in the town square and took them back to my family member's house in the village first, then later to the farm. That's when I woke up. My dream never had a resolution.

I decided to write the story so I could decide how it ended. I like that Kenz is still herself at the end of the story.

I hope you enjoyed this short tale.

I've got another 'game' sort of books in the works, a cozy mystery trilogy that has a first draft for each book, and a plot outline for a cozy fantasy. There's lots coming. I know not every book is for everyone, but I've decided this pen name is one that will let me do a few things I've been wanting to do that I can't write with my more well established pen name that includes books for a very specific community of readers.

Happy reading, everyone!

~ M. A. Hagan

About M.A. Hagan

M.A. Hagan creates family-friendly game books and cozy fantasy and mystery stories. The game books offer clean, engaging activities for children and families to enjoy together, from wholesome Truth or Dare prompts to group challenges that spark laughter and connection. M .A.'s cozy stories unfold in gentle worlds where conflicts resolve over coffee, tea, or books and the biggest mysteries involve misplaced enchantments and closely held secrets.

The pen name M.A. Hagan represents a focused exploration of family entertainment, cozy fantasy and light mysteries, complementing her broader literary works published as Anne Hagan. When not developing new group activities or crafting cozy communities, M.A. enjoys testing games on her own family.

www.ingramcontent.com/pod-product-compliance
Lightning Source LLC
LaVergne TN
LVHW010104110826
845155LV00028B/473

* 9 7 8 1 9 5 0 8 2 8 3 3 3 *